DARK TERROR

Kelly was vaguely aware of the cold sweat covering her body, of her uncontrolled shivers, of her heart thundering in her chest.

She knew she shouldn't stay here. Part of her wanted to turn and run, but something kept her from moving.

Kelly heard a footstep behind her and whirled around. *"Who's there?"* she gasped.

She didn't see anyone. Then a voice came from the deepest shadows behind a tall stone monument.

"He's dead, isn't he?"

Other Avon Flare Books by
Carol Gorman

DIE FOR ME

GRAVEYARD MOON

CAROL GORMAN

AN AVON FLARE BOOK

Thanks to Jodi Mangrich and Ron Heither
at the Village Market for their help.

GRAVEYARD MOON is an original publication of Avon Books. This work has never before appeared in book form.

AVON BOOKS
A division of
The Hearst Corporation
1350 Avenue of the Americas
New York, New York 10019

Copyright © 1993 by Carol Gorman
Published by arrangement with the author
Library of Congress Catalog Card Number: 92-93926
ISBN: 0-380-76991-3
RL: 5.3

First Avon Flare Printing: April 1993

AVON FLARE TRADEMARK REG. U.S. PAT. OFF. AND IN OTHER COUNTRIES, MARCA REGISTRADA, HECHO EN U.S.A.

Printed in the U.S.A.

RA 10 9 8 7 6 5 4 3 2 1

For my friend, Kate Aspengren,
who makes me laugh over lunch
in Iowa City.

Chapter 1

In a horror movie last year, Kelly McLees had seen a decomposed corpse. Most of its flesh had been eaten away by lice and maggots, leaving little more of the face than a grinning shell.

Now, stumbling through the darkness of the graveyard after the three girls ahead of her, she thought of that movie again. She couldn't help thinking that under the stone markers outlined in the moonlight were decomposing bodies like the one she'd seen on the screen.

Kelly shivered in the cold and forced the image from her mind. She gripped the can of beer that Alice Roe had shoved in her hand a few minutes ago and kept up the pace behind her three companions.

"I thought you were going to bring a flashlight," Alice whispered irritably. She was a senior at Kelly's new school, Spencer Point High. Her complaint was targeted at Tracy Wilcox, also a senior.

"You said *you'd* bring it," Tracy said, shifting her bulging backpack to one side.

"I did *not*," Alice snapped. "I brought the beer! *I* took the chance buying it with the fake ID! The least you could've done was bring a flashlight!"

"Come on, you guys," said Colette Glass. She was

a junior in Kelly's lit class. "It'll be scarier in the dark anyway. A whole night in the graveyard! This'll be fun!"

"At least I remembered the beer," said Alice. "I can have fun *anywhere* if I've got enough beer."

Fun? Kelly thought. A cold, drunken night in the graveyard? These girls had a strange way of having fun. She folded her arms across her chest in the chilly night air to try and keep warm.

A full moon overhead, shining over the autumn-stripped trees and cold granite headstones, cast eerie shadows that stretched ominously along the ground. Kelly knew she was too old to be frightened by the darkness of a graveyard. It's just that everything to-night was so unfamiliar, so strange: the three girls, the beer, and surrounding them in all directions were tombstones marking where the dead lay.

"I like this place," Alice said. "It's kind of creepy. But then, that's why we came." She glanced over her shoulder at Kelly. "Just the right place for a party."

Tracy laughed. Colette touched Kelly's arm and gave her a reassuring squeeze.

Kelly knew this was some kind of test. Alice and Tracy were sizing her up to see if she would fit in with them.

Colette already liked her, that was obvious from the first day of school. Kelly knew this party wasn't Colette's idea. She just hoped she could take a few gulps of the beer and let the others drink the rest. She'd never been drunk before and didn't want to try it now.

Kelly had lived here less than a month and badly missed her old friends back home. She'd moved to Spencer Point with her grandparents, who raised her after her parents had died in a car accident when she was a baby.

Grandad's heart attack last year had forced him

and Nana to pause in their busy lives and reassess their goals. Now in their seventies, Grandad and Nana had decided to return to Spencer Point and spend the rest of their lives in the town where they'd both been born and raised. They'd even bought Grandad's childhood home, an old farmhouse on a small acreage seven miles from town.

Kelly had ached with loneliness for the first two weeks and ran up expensive long-distance bills to her friends, who lived more than four hundred miles away. But gradually she realized that if she wanted to find any happiness in Spencer Point, she was going to have to make new friends.

That's how she happened to be groping her way through a graveyard at eleven o'clock on a Friday night. She'd told her grandparents she was spending the night with Colette. She hadn't wanted to tell them the whole truth. They certainly wouldn't have approved of this party among the tombstones.

The girls had told her to bring nothing but the clothes on her back. They'd provide everything she needed. They all wore backpacks strapped to their shoulders stuffed with blankets, beer, soda, and junk food.

"Don't worry, Kelly," said Alice. Kelly could see her sly smile in the dim moonlight. "We're perfectly safe out here unless there's a murderer or rapist hiding behind one of these trees. Or maybe a ghost. The graveyard is haunted, you know."

Tracy spoke up. "That's true. There're lots of stories about ghosts roaming around out here. One is of a headless man who was decapitated about fifteen years ago. His killer was never found. Neither was his head."

Alice snickered.

Kelly didn't respond. She knew that Alice and

3

Tracy were baiting her, trying to make her nervous or angry or scared. Kelly wasn't sure which. She wasn't really frightened, but she didn't feel very sure of herself either. These girls, especially Alice, weren't like her friends back home.

The girls made their way slowly into the center of the graveyard, carefully stepping around the headstones.

A footstep sounded behind them. Kelly turned and stared into the darkness.

"What was that?" she whispered.

"What?" Alice said, turning to her. "I didn't hear anything."

"Behind those bushes," Kelly said, keeping her voice low.

"Maybe it's the headless ghost," Tracy said. She laughed.

"Or a serial killer," said Alice. She didn't laugh.

"Didn't you hear it?" Kelly asked Colette.

In the dim light, Colette shook her head.

Maybe she was imagining things. Could two swallows of beer do that to a person?

No, of course not.

She didn't want to look foolish, but she was *sure* she'd heard something.

"I think someone's over there," Kelly said. "Hiding behind that bush."

"Waiting to kill you," Alice said. She stared at Kelly in the dim light.

Kelly felt a surge of anger rush through her and she glared back at Alice.

A long moment passed. Then Colette grabbed Kelly's arm. "Come on," she said. "Let's find a place to have our party."

"Look," Tracy whispered, pointing into the distance ahead of them.

Looming up out of the gloom was a building. It wasn't large. In fact it wasn't much bigger than a shack, but in the middle of the graveyard, with only the moon lighting it dimly from above, the place looked dark and foreboding.

"It's the caretaker's house," Alice whispered.

Maybe it's the caretaker behind the bush, Kelly thought. She glanced behind her again. She couldn't see anyone standing there, but she *felt* his presence. He was watching them, she was sure of it.

"Does somebody really live in that house?" Colette asked.

"I don't know," said Alice. "Let's find out."

Colette grabbed Alice's arm. "You can't just walk in there. Maybe the caretaker's asleep."

Alice jerked her arm away. "Maybe the place is empty."

"Maybe," Kelly said, with another glance over her shoulder at the shadowy form of the bush, "he wouldn't like us barging into his house."

"There's only one way to find out." Alice led the way to the small door.

"Come on, Alice," whispered Colette. "We were going to spend the night in the graveyard. Nobody said anything about bothering some poor old guy—"

"Shhh!" Alice rapped sharply on the small, wooden door. The noise echoed through the silent graveyard.

The door hadn't been shut securely, and it swung open slowly on creaking hinges.

"Let's get out of here, Alice," said Tracy. She sounded nervous. "This is creepy."

Alice turned to face the others. "I'm going inside. You cowards can do whatever you want."

"Don't, Alice!" Colette whispered urgently.

"Maybe somebody's inside. I mean, *anybody* could be in there!"

Alice didn't answer. She pushed the door wide open and peered inside the small house.

"What's in there?" whispered Tracy.

Alice edged her way into the house and disappeared into the darkness. There was a long silence.

"Alice?" whispered Tracy.

"Come on out now, Alice," said Colette. "You've proved you're braver than we are."

There was no answer.

"Alice?"

"Come on," Tracy said. "She's just trying to scare us. Let's leave her in there. She'll come out when she gets bored enough."

Kelly remained frozen to her spot. She didn't know if it was the image of the corpse from the horror movie or the talk of headless ghosts or the frightening thought that someone was watching them from behind the tall bush. Whatever the reason, she was frightened. Alice had walked into the small, dark house and not returned. She didn't really like Alice, but Kelly didn't want to see her hurt either.

If this were a horror movie, there would be a serial killer inside who would chop Alice up into bloody little pieces, Kelly thought.

Oh, stop, she told herself. This isn't a horror movie. This is real life.

But awful things happen in real life, too, don't they? Maybe there *was* someone inside, someone who'd hurt Alice. They couldn't just walk away and leave her there. Especially not with someone so close, watching.

Why was he here? *What did he want from them?*

Kelly stepped over to the doorway. "Alice?" she whispered. "You okay?"

Inside the house, there was a heavy *thud*. Alice swore in the darkness.

"Alice!" Colette cried. "What's going on?"

"I can't *see*, that's what's going on!" Alice shouted.

"Would this help?" Tracy asked, stepping forward. With a flick of her finger, a small flame burst to life at the edge of a silver cigarette lighter.

Alice reappeared in the doorway. "*Now* you offer the light?" she said sourly. "I just banged my shins on something big in there. And hard."

"Sorry," Tracy said. "I'd forgotten I brought it."

Alice grabbed the lighter and turned back into the house. This time the girls followed her. The interior of the house was still dark, but the cigarette lighter provided enough light to see a few feet in front of them.

The house didn't hold normal household furnishings, but instead was filled with outdoor maintenance equipment: a lawnmower, weed trimmer, hoses wrapped in loose coils, hoes, tree-trimming equipment, and smaller hand tools—an axe, hammer, and saw—lined the edge of the room.

"Nobody lives here," whispered Tracy.

"No kidding," said Alice sarcastically. She rested her hand on a large barrel. "This is what I just bumped into."

"I wonder why the house wasn't locked," said Colette. "Anybody could walk in and steal all this stuff."

"Someone must have forgotten to lock it up," Kelly said.

Alice turned to face the girls. The flame of the lighter was just under her chin, distorting her features with odd shadows and giving her an ugly, sinister appearance.

"Let's spend the night here," she said. Her mouth,

above the flickering light, curled up at the edges, and her teeth looked pointed and black.

"In here?" Tracy said. "I'd rather be outside under the stars."

"Me too," said Colette.

"Yeah, me too," said Kelly.

"Guess you're outvoted, Alice," said Colette.

"Well, at least we can eat our food in here," Alice said. "Get me another beer." She turned to Tracy. "Hold the light, will you?"

She handed Tracy the lighter, threw off her backpack, unzipped it, and pulled out a blanket. Colette handed her a can of beer. "Get comfortable, everyone."

Alice spread the blanket on the floor, collapsed on top of it, and popped the top off her beer. The girls sat down cross-legged on the blanket.

"Beer for everyone," said Alice. She pulled out two six-packs and one liter bottle of Coke.

Tracy and Colette opened their packs and brought out bags of chips, dips, and deli sandwiches.

"Great," said Colette. "I'm starved."

"I hope the caretaker doesn't come while we're here," Colette said.

Kelly turned to look around the small house. The tiny flame of the cigarette lighter that Tracy still held didn't begin to illuminate the dark corners. The house was filled with blackness and gloom. There appeared to be only one way in or out. What if the person hiding behind the bush suddenly threw open the door and blocked their exit? She didn't feel safe in the house at all.

"Is there much crime around here?" she asked, consciously keeping her voice light. "I mean, in Spencer Point?"

"No," said Colette. "Not much."

8

"There've been some break-ins over the last year in the wealthy neighborhoods," said Tracy. "But it's been a couple of years since we've had a murder."

"About time for another one," said Alice with a little smile.

What a jerk, Kelly thought, staring at Alice. You would never know to look at her that she was such a nasty person. She was small and blond and pretty. It was only when she opened her mouth that all the ugliness came out.

"There was a hit-and-run last year," said Colette. "A kid in the senior class was killed."

"That's awful," Kelly said.

"The driver was never found." Colette's voice was sad. "Daryl—he was the kid who was killed—he was kind of strange. Still, it was a horrible tragedy."

Alice glanced back over her shoulder. "What's *that?*" she said, her voice in a rising crescendo.

She jerked the lighter out of Tracy's hand and thrust it into the darkness behind her. She let out a scream that sent an electric charge up Kelly's back.

"A snake! A *snake!*"

Alice threw up her arms, screaming hysterically, scrambled to her feet, and fled from the small house. She'd taken the lighter with her, so the room was suddenly consumed by the blackness of night.

Shouts and shrieks filled the house as the girls stumbled through the dark toward the open door. Kelly had seen plenty of harmless snakes in the ravine near her old home, but she didn't like them and certainly didn't want to stay in a dark room with one. Besides, there was no way of knowing for sure whether this one was harmless or not.

She grabbed the blanket from the floor, scrambled to her feet, and ran out the door.

Kelly found Tracy and Colette a short distance

from the house. They were breathing hard and talking in shaky voices.

"Where's Alice?" Kelly asked.

"She ran on," said Tracy. "She's over by the black angel."

"The black angel?"

"A sculpture. It's made of wrought iron or something."

"Boy, Alice sure was scared of that snake!" Colette said. She giggled nervously. "The only times I've heard screams like that were in horror movies."

"Yeah," said Tracy. "I didn't think Alice was afraid of anything."

After sitting in the darkness of the little house, the moon suspended over the graveyard seemed unusually bright, beaming a silvery haze over the tombstones.

Kelly peered into the distance and saw the silhouette of the black angel statue. It stood with its wings spread, as if in flight, its head held high, gazing into the distance as if it were ascending to someplace beautiful. Standing below the angel, her arms wrapped protectively around herself, stood Alice.

"Come on," Colette said. "Let's see how Alice is doing."

The girls threaded their way around gravestones and over to Alice.

"You okay?" Colette said.

"I *hate* snakes! I *loathe* them!" Alice was trembling all over.

"What's so scary about snakes?" said Tracy. "I mean, they're creepy, but I thought there was an ax murderer behind you in there! Your scream could've wakened the dead."

"So to speak." Colette grinned and looked around

the graveyard. "I don't see any formerly dead people climbing out of graves around here."

"Shut up, Colette," Alice snapped. She turned away, still breathing hard, and put her face in her hands.

"Sorry," Colette said.

The girls stood awkwardly, not knowing what to say.

"You okay?" Colette asked in a quiet voice. She put a hand on Alice's shoulder, but Alice batted it off and stalked away. Her breath came in little gasps.

"I *hate* snakes!" she said again. "I *hate* them!"

"So do I," said Colette softly.

"My brother used to find bull snakes in the weeds behind his friend's house," Alice said, her voice barely under control. "He terrorized me with them. Once on my birthday he gave me a present wrapped with a pretty pink bow and when I opened the box, there was a—a—a three-foot-long bull snake inside. It was coiled like a rattler ready to spring with its tongue flicking out at me." She trembled violently, but Kelly couldn't tell whether from fear or anger.

"It's okay, Alice," Colette reassured her.

"Let's find a spot to relax," said Tracy.

"This is a good place," said Colette. "I like the angel."

She took the blanket that Kelly had grabbed from the floor of the house and spread it on the ground. She sat down. "Where's the rest of the stuff?" she asked.

"Here," said Tracy.

The girls hadn't managed to get everything off the floor in their desperate escape from the house, but they had three blankets, several packages of chips, and the two six-packs of beer among them.

"This'll do," Colette said. "Sit down, everybody." She looked up at Alice. "Come on, Alice."

Alice remained standing and turned away from the others with her arms wrapped around herself.

"Have a beer, Alice," Tracy said.

Alice slowly turned and accepted the beer.

"One for you," Tracy said and handed Kelly her second can of beer that night—the first long forgotten in the caretaker's shed.

Alice still looked a little glassy-eyed, but she sank to the blanket.

"Who's got the first ghost story?" Colette asked.

"I've got one," said Tracy.

"Let's hear it," Alice said quietly.

Tracy told an old camp tale about two kids getting lost in the woods and coming upon a scary old man with a razor-sharp ax. Kelly had heard the story several times as a kid, but Tracy told it so well, adding weird details of her own, that it seemed new and almost as frightening as when she was eight.

The wind began to blow at the end of Tracy's story, a low moaning through the trees, and the girls huddled closer under the blanket.

"Do you believe in ghosts?" Tracy asked.

"I do," answered Colette. "I believe the soul lives on after we die, so why not believe in ghosts? Maybe they're lost spirits who can't find their way to heaven."

"Or hell," said Alice.

Kelly had felt sorry for her when she'd been trembling in fear of the snake. But now that Alice was beginning to relax, Kelly saw the girl returning to her normal, unpleasant self.

"Have another beer," Alice said, pushing another can of beer at Kelly.

"Thanks, but I've had enough. By the way, where do we go to the bathroom around here?"

Alice raised herself up on her knees. "See the tree over there?"

She pointed to a gnarled tree in the distance. Under the graveyard moon, the tree appeared in silhouette, its branches reaching, like a pleading old man, into the sky.

"Go there. Just to the other side of the tree."

Kelly looked around expectantly, hoping someone would offer to go with her. No one did.

What if the person behind the bushes had followed them to the black angel?

"Okay." Kelly didn't want to give Alice the satisfaction of knowing that she was spooked, so she got up and made her way toward the tree, alone.

"Don't wake up the ghosts!" Alice hollered after her. "They'll haunt you all night if you do!"

For the thousandth time since she moved to Spencer Point, Kelly felt a pang of longing for her old friends. *If only we hadn't moved here!* she thought. *I hate this town.*

She approached the tree in the dim light of the moon. Just to the other side of the tree, Alice had said.

Kelly stepped around the tree where the ground sloped down into a gloomy darkness.

Something on the ground at the edge of the shadows caught her eye. Something lying there. Something very still.

She squinted into the inky blackness and all at once realized what she was seeing. Her stomach lurched. She cried out in a low wail.

Sprawled in the ditch was a body.

It was a boy, dressed in a plaid shirt splattered with blood. His face was turned toward Kelly, and in the dim light of the moon, she could see his eyes staring sightlessly up at her, his mouth open, permanently fixed in an expression of unspeakable horror.

Chapter 2

Kelly's hand flew to her mouth. She heard another low moan and was surprised when she realized the mournful sounds had come from her own throat.

A twig snapped behind her and she whirled around.

"Who's there?" she gasped.

She didn't see anyone. Then a voice came from the deepest shadows behind a tall stone monument.

"He's dead, isn't he?"

Kelly didn't stop to think. Her heart thundered in her ears.

She cried out, turned, and ran as fast as she could across the graveyard, toward the other girls, the black angel, and—she hoped—safety.

She tripped over a short grave marker in the dark, hitting one knee painfully on the ground. She scrambled to her feet and kept running.

The girls were sitting where she'd left them.

"What's wrong?" Alice had seen her coming first and rose to her feet.

The other girls stood up, their eyes big, as Kelly stumbled over to them.

"There's—there's a guy—" Kelly stammered,

gasping for breath. She pointed toward the gnarled tree in the distance.

"What's wrong?" Alice said. "Calm down."

"A boy." Kelly began again. She was quivering all over. "He's dead. He's *dead.*"

"What?" Alice said. "What are you talking about?"

"I saw a body by the tree," Kelly said. "A guy about our age. He's *dead!*"

"A dead body?" Tracy said. "Are you sure?"

"Of course I'm sure!" Kelly cried.

"But it's so dark," Tracy said. "How could you see—"

"I could *see* it!" Kelly insisted. "By the light of the moon. It—*he*—he was splattered with blood! And someone else was there, too."

"Someone else?" Alice said. "Who?"

"In the shadows," Kelly said, hiccoughing. "I don't know who it was."

There was a long silence. Kelly, still panting, focused her gaze on Alice, who stood before her. Alice stared back at her, her head cocked to one side.

Kelly realized then what Alice was thinking.

"You don't believe me, do you?" she cried. *"Why would I make up a story like that?"*

"Maybe because I kidded you about being afraid of the ghosts?" Alice said. Even in the dim light, Kelly could see Alice's eyebrow raised. "You paying me back, Kelly?"

Kelly's mouth dropped open. *"Of course not!* If you don't believe me, come see for yourself! No, that's too dangerous. Someone's there, behind the monument. We should go to the police!"

"No way," said Alice. "Kelly, you're pushing this game of yours way too far."

"It's not a game!"

"I won't go to the police," Alice said calmly.

"Then come to the tree with me. See him for yourself. Maybe it'll be safe if we all go."

No one spoke. She looked pleadingly at Colette. *"You'll* come with me, won't you?"

"Well, I think we should all go," said Alice calmly. "But I still don't believe you. What do you guys think?"

"I think we should go and see," said Colette.

Alice shrugged. "So let's go."

Kelly sighed with relief and started quickly back across the graveyard.

"Come on," she called urgently. "Hurry!"

"If there's really a dead body there, he's not going anywhere," Alice said.

When they reached the gnarled tree, Kelly gestured toward the shadows.

"Over here," she said. "In the ditch."

She hurried around the tree and stopped short.

The body was gone.

"So where's the stiff?" Alice said, coming up behind her.

Kelly, her body rigid, pointed to the spot. "Here. It was here."

"Uh-huh," said Alice.

"It was here!" cried Kelly. "He was lying in the ditch, splattered with blood!"

Alice grinned triumphantly at Tracy and Colette. "Nice try, but you can see we didn't go for it."

"But he was here! He was dead! His eyes were open and staring straight at me, he was covered with blood—"

Alice turned and started back toward the black angel. "Come on, you guys," she said over her shoulder. "Excitement's over. Let's get back under the blanket. "It's getting cold out here."

16

Kelly stared after her dumbly. Tracy was already starting off in the same direction.

What was going on here?

Colette put a hand on Kelly's shoulder. "Come on," she said softly. "Let's go back."

"But, Colette," Kelly said. "There really *was* a body here. And someone spoke to me. He was standing behind that monument." She stared at the tall slab of stone. It was enshrouded in deep shadows.

Was he still there?

"Stay here just a minute more," Kelly said to Colette. *"Please?"*

"Okay."

Her heart beating a steady tattoo in her chest, she stepped slowly over to the monument. The wind moaned through the trees overhead while Kelly peered into the darkness, trying to make her eyes penetrate the small patch of night behind the tall stone.

All was still. There was no movement behind the monument.

"He's gone."

Colette's voice was soft. "Let's go back."

"But I swear the body was here."

"Okay," Colette said. "But it's not here now. So let's go back—"

"Don't you believe me?"

A pained look came over Colette's face. "Yeah," she said. "But I don't know what to do about it. It's not here now."

"But what could have happened to it?"

"I don't know," Colette said. "Come on."

Colette gave her a gentle nudge, and numbly, Kelly started moving toward the other girls.

"I just don't get it," Kelly mumbled. "The man in the shadows must have taken it away."

"Maybe," said Colette.

"It *had* to be that way," Kelly said. "The man behind the monument must have been the killer. He dragged the body away after I ran to get you guys."

"Sounds reasonable."

"Colette, we have to go to the police," Kelly said. Colette didn't respond.

"We have to tell them about the murder!"

Still Colette was quiet.

"Colette!"

Colette kept walking. "But there's nothing to tell them. I mean, you thought you saw a dead body, but there's no body there now. There's no evidence for them at all."

"I didn't just *think* I saw a body—"

They arrived at the black angel, where Alice and Tracy were waiting.

"We have to go to the police," Kelly insisted. "Even though the body disappeared, we have to report the murder."

"Kelly, we're not idiots," said Alice. "You can drop this charade of yours. There's no body, there was no murder, and the game's over. We didn't buy it! Okay?"

"But someone was behind the tall monument," Kelly insisted. "He must have killed the boy and then dragged him away after I left."

"I don't think there was a body there in the first place," said Alice.

"I don't either," said Tracy.

"But *you* believe me," Kelly said to Colette.

Colette hesitated and glanced at Alice, who glared at her.

"I don't think going to the police makes sense," Colette said. "There's nothing for them to see."

Kelly stared at the girls in disbelief. "So we're not

going to do *anything?* We're going to let a murder go unreported?"

"We're going to let a dead body that you *made up* go unreported," said Alice.

"Come on," said Colette. "Let's get back under the blanket."

Kelly watched the three girls seat themselves on the ground and spread the blanket over them.

"Come on, Kelly," Colette coaxed. "It's cold."

"Why don't we go home, then," she asked.

Alice replied, "Oh, grow up, Kelly. There's no body. We're here and we're spending the night."

There was a war going on in Kelly's mind. One half screamed that she should go to the police and tell her story, whether there was any evidence or not. The other half argued that if she went to the authorities now they wouldn't find a body and she'd lose the only friends she'd made since moving to Spencer Point.

She certainly didn't consider Alice a friend. But the other two were okay, especially Colette. Colette seemed to be torn between her loyalty to Alice and her new friend Kelly.

Colette looked up at her and smiled a little. "Come on, Kelly," she repeated. "It's cold."

This isn't right, Kelly thought. *We should go to the police.*

But Colette was right about one thing. There was no evidence. If these three girls didn't believe her story, why would the police believe it?

They *wouldn't* believe it, she knew, and they'd probably think she was crazy.

She sat down next to Colette on the ground and covered herself with the blanket. She wouldn't do anything right now. Maybe, before the night was over, she would decide whether or not to report what she saw.

It was a long night. Kelly didn't sleep much. With only three blankets between the four of them, it was hard to keep warm. More than that, she couldn't get the dead boy out of her mind.

Who was he? Why had he been killed? Had she seen his murderer, the man behind the monument?

She really hadn't *seen* him. He was completely hidden in the shadows. But she had heard his voice. He'd spoken to her.

Kelly tossed on the hard ground, trying to get comfortable. Finally, she gave up and sat up on the blanket, leaning against a tree. If I had my car, she thought, I'd have driven myself home by now. The girls were too far out of town to walk home.

The morning dawned with gray skies and a chill wind blowing from the north. Kelly and the girls collected their things to go home.

She'd made it through the night. She didn't know if they'd accepted her as their friend. But she was so tired and cold right now, she didn't care.

Kelly said good-bye after they drove the seven miles to her grandparents' house to drop her off.

She greeted Grandad and Nana, who were in the kitchen sitting before steaming bowls of oatmeal.

"Hi, honey," called Nana. She smiled and smoothed her gray hair with curled, arthritic fingers. "Did you have a nice time?"

"Yeah," Kelly lied. "It was fine."

Why bother them with a story about a disappearing dead body? They'd only be alarmed—and understandably upset that she'd lied to them about where she'd been all night.

"Come and warm up your insides, girl," Grandad

said. His chubby cheeks were naturally rosy, and with his white hair, he only needed a beard and moustache to look just like Santa Claus.

"Thanks, guys, but I'm not very hungry. We didn't sleep a lot, so I think I'll just go up to my room and take a nap."

"Rest well, dear," Nana said.

Kelly climbed the stairs to her room, slipped out of her clothes, and crawled under the covers. She reached over and flicked on the electric blanket.

Kelly snuggled down into the warming covers. She was very tired and within a few minutes her mind had numbed and she felt herself drifting toward sleep.

She didn't know how long she had slept when the phone rang.

Nana'll get it, she thought.

The phone rang again, but stopped abruptly. She was just drifting back to sleep when there was a soft tap on the door.

"Kelly?" Her grandmother's round face peeked through the cracked door. "The phone's for you. I told her you were resting, but she insisted on talking to you."

Kelly rolled over. "Thanks, Nana." She reached sleepily for the phone next to her bed.

Nana nodded, stepped back into the hall, and closed the bedroom door.

"Hello?"

"Kelly, this is Colette." She sounded upset, close to tears.

"Hi."

"Kelly, something *awful* has happened! We've got to talk to you about last night! You were *right*. The boy you found in the graveyard—he was *murdered!*"

Chapter 3

Kelly explained to her grandparents that a friend needed to see her about school. Then she hurried out to the old barn, where she parked her eight-year-old station wagon.

She backed out of the barn, angling the car's backside to the right, turned around, and drove down the gravel lane to the highway that led into Spencer Point. She was grateful for the used car that Grandad had given to her on her sixteenth birthday. It allowed her the freedom to come and go whenever she wished.

She arrived at the city park about fifteen minutes later and pulled into the parking area next to the children's playground. Alice, Tracy, and Colette were already there, pacing around the empty concrete wading pool.

Kelly got out of the car and walked over to the pool.

The three girls glanced around at one another, as if they didn't know which of them would tell her.

"Did you see the morning paper?" said Colette finally. She had a folded newspaper under her arm.

"No."

"You were right," Colette said. "There was a murder last night. A junior named Craig Harris."

"I *told* you!"

"I know," Colette said. "We—we're really sorry that we didn't do anything. We—" Her voice faded and she turned away.

"What?"

"We did something awful to you," Colette said.

"It was just sort of an initiation," Tracy whined.

"We didn't know it would really happen," Alice said, stiffly.

"What are you *talking* about?"

Colette stepped forward. "I've never been so ashamed of anything in my life," she said. "Kelly, you know the boy you found in the ditch at the graveyard?"

"Yeah."

"It was all a terrible hoax."

"We talked Craig into posing as a dead person," Colette said.

"To scare you," said Tracy.

"We told him to splatter himself with ketchup and lie in the ditch until you found him," Colette said. "That's why Alice—why we pushed all that beer at you last night. So you'd have to go to the bathroom and then you'd find him there by the tree. I was sorry we'd dreamed this up as soon as we got to the graveyard—"

"So this Craig wasn't really dead?" Kelly asked.

"No," said Colette. "I mean, I don't know. He was supposed to get away after you ran to get us."

"Why?"

"Because—so we could accuse you of making it up," said Colette. She glared at Alice, then turned back to Kelly. "Pretty rotten trick, wasn't it?"

Kelly didn't answer.

"But somebody really *did* kill Craig!" cried Tracy. "That wasn't part of the plan!"

"His body was found clear across town in an empty parking lot about two o'clock this morning," said Colette. "His throat was slashed."

She handed Kelly the paper. It was the headline story on the front page. Kelly scanned the article, looked at Craig's picture, then handed the paper back to Colette.

"That's him," she said. "Only he was wearing a plaid shirt and blue jeans." She shook her head. "Poor guy."

"We're responsible for his death," said Colette grimly.

"We are *not*," Alice snapped. "Craig was alive at the graveyard."

"How can you be sure?" said Colette. "Maybe somebody killed him before Kelly got there."

Kelly shook her head. "His throat wasn't slashed. The blood—ketchup—was on his shirt. He was staring, open-eyed, but his neck wasn't bloody."

"So he was faking it," said Alice. "He was killed afterward. After he left the graveyard. So we're *not* responsible!"

"But there was someone hiding behind that tall monument," said Kelly. "Maybe—"

"Maybe it was the murderer!" said Colette. "Maybe he followed Craig after he left the graveyard and killed him."

"Oh, this is all so sick!" cried Tracy.

"We'd better all go together to the police," said Kelly.

"The police!" cried Tracy.

"No police," said Alice.

"What do you mean, no police?" said Kelly. "A boy's been murdered!"

24

"The cops'll blame *us* for the murder!" said Tracy. "We made Craig play a corpse just a few hours before he was killed for real! We could be charged with accessory to murder."

"But you weren't involved in his death," said Kelly.

"The cops won't believe that!" said Tracy.

"Craig wasn't dead when he was at the graveyard," Alice said smoothly. "So there's no reason to go to the police."

Kelly frowned. "But if his murderer followed him from the graveyard—"

"We don't *know* that!" Alice said.

"Who *else* would be hiding behind the monument?"

"What about this man you saw?" Colette said. "What did he look like?"

"I couldn't see his face," Kelly said. "He was completely hidden in the shadows."

"But he spoke to you?"

"Yes. He said, 'He's dead, isn't he?' "

"Why would a murderer tell you that Craig was dead *before* he killed him?" said Alice.

"I don't know," said Kelly. "Why was the man there in the first place?"

"None of this makes sense," said Tracy.

"Anyway, we're not going to the police," Alice said. "Let's wait and see what happens. Maybe the cops'll find out who did it, and we won't have to get involved."

Kelly eyed Alice scornfully. "You don't want to get *involved?*"

"I don't want my life ruined, okay? I'm applying for scholarships all over the country. I can't afford to blow it!"

Kelly stared at Alice, then looked around at the others.

"I won't go to the police *yet,*" she said softly. "But if the murderer hasn't been caught in a week, I'm going to tell them what I know."

"Which is *nothing!*" Alice said contemptuously.

"Maybe. But the little bit of information that I *do* have might be a missing piece of the puzzle. It might help them solve—"

"Let's get out of here," Alice interrupted. "I'm sick of talking about murder and dead bodies. Come on, Tracy."

"Yeah," said Tracy. She headed with Alice toward her car. "You coming, Colette?"

"I drove my own car," Colette reminded her. "But I'm going to stay a minute with Kelly."

"Suit yourself." Alice shrugged.

Alice and Tracy climbed into the car and left the park.

"Kelly, I'm so sorry about this whole mess," Colette said. "And about what we did to you."

"I don't care about the trick you pulled on me," said Kelly. "After all, I survived. I'm *alive.* I just keep thinking about that poor guy. I keep wondering if just being in the graveyard last night put him in the wrong place at the wrong time. Maybe he was killed because of my initiation."

Colette sat down on the edge of the wading pool and buried her head in her hands.

"I know. I keep thinking the same thing. Poor Craig. He was such a nice guy! He was in my history class at school. And he worked at the Corner Market with me." Her voice broke and she sniffed. "I should've stood up to those girls. I didn't want to play that stupid trick on you! I hated seeing you so upset—I felt so guilty!"

Kelly walked over and sat next to Colette. "It isn't your fault. Nobody knew someone was stalking Craig." The girls fell silent. Kelly put her arm around Colette's shoulder and sighed. Finally she said, "Can I ask you something? What's with Alice, anyway? Why is she so popular? She bosses everyone around and they do whatever she wants."

"Yeah, I know," said Colette. "Including me." She shook her head. "I don't know. She's gorgeous, she's pushy, she's—she's got power around school, that's for sure."

"Do you like her?"

"Let's say I don't exactly respect her," said Colette. "She *can* be fun, though, sometimes. We got to be friends at the Market. She works there, too. I just hate to cross her. She really knows how to make your life miserable if she wants to."

A movement, something in blue, caught Kelly's attention out of the corner of her eye. She turned and focused her gaze on a stand of trees at the edge of the park.

A guy stood there dressed in a worn denim jacket and blue jeans with holes in the knees. He looked a little older than Kelly, with dark hair and dark eyes.

He was leaning against a tree, watching her.

A chill ran up Kelly's back. There was something about his gaze. It was so dark, so penetrating.

Kelly turned to Colette. "Who's that?" she said in a low voice.

"Who?"

Without looking back, Kelly nodded slightly toward the boy. "He's standing over to your left, in the trees."

Colette looked. "I don't see anyone."

Kelly turned back.

The guy was gone.

27

"He was there a second ago," Kelly said. "Leaning against the tree."

Colette shrugged. "Beats me."

Kelly watched a moment longer, waiting to see if he'd reappear.

She saw nothing.

Kelly sighed again. "I'm so tired. I'm going home to bed. See you later."

"Okay."

Colette got in her Ford and Kelly climbed into her old station wagon. Colette pulled out first, waved at Kelly, then drove off out of the parking area.

Kelly followed. As she neared the trees where she'd seen the boy, she slowed down and scanned the area for a dark head or a blue denim jacket.

But the park was empty. No one was there.

She shrugged, then yawned widely. She was too tired to think of graveyards or Alice or a mysterious guy in the park. Or even poor Craig.

She pulled onto the street and headed toward home.

Chapter 4

Everyone at school on Monday was talking about Craig's murder. It had been reported in the paper that he'd told his mother about ten-thirty he was going to meet somebody. He hadn't said who he was meeting, but she had assumed it was a friend from school. Most of the talk on Monday morning was speculation about who Craig had gone to meet.

Kelly, of course, knew who he was going to meet. He was going to meet *her* in the graveyard, after first splattering himself with ketchup and sprawling in the ditch.

Kelly felt guilty that she knew what only three other people in the world—or four, counting the man behind the monument—knew about where he'd gone that night. The only thing that made her feel better was her promise to herself that at the end of the week, if the murderer hadn't been caught, she would go to the police and tell them what had happened.

At lunch Kelly sat with Colette, Tracy, Alice, and some other girls who were all talking about the murder.

"I can't imagine anybody wanting to kill Craig," said a junior in Kelly's math class. "He was such a

29

quiet guy. I mean, he's not the type who'd get into a fight."

"I know," said her friend. "Remember that time he was on his way to Randy Owen's party and he found that dog that had been hit by a car? He couldn't find the dog's owner, so he took it to the vet himself and paid the doctor to put the dog's leg in a cast."

"I remember that," said Tracy. "Everybody he was supposed to take to the party was mad because he never showed up."

"Then he explained to everyone, and we were *still* mad!" said Alice. "He should've called to explain."

"He was so upset about the dog, he forgot about the party," said Colette. "I remember hearing that story. He kept the dog, didn't he?"

"I think so," said the first girl.

"Craig must've had a soft heart," Kelly said.

She looked over at Alice, who glared back at her.

Kelly stabbed at a piece of chicken casserole on her lunch tray. She wasn't interested in eating. All she could think about was Craig, a boy she'd never met, who was becoming more real for her all the time. A boy who was killed after agreeing to play a corpse for Kelly's initiation.

She was possibly the last person to see him alive.

Except for his killer.

The girls at her table kept talking about the murder, but Kelly only listened with half an ear. Her elbow propped up on the table, she leaned her cheek on her hand and sighed deeply as a wave of sadness washed over her. She wished she could have known Craig, a boy who'd stop to help a wounded dog on the highway. He must have been a special person.

She glanced absentmindedly across the cafeteria, and her gaze fell on a dark-haired guy who was staring right at her.

The guy from the park.

He was holding his lunch tray and moving toward the edge of the room. He nodded slightly to Kelly and sat down at the long cafeteria table. No one was with him. He was eating alone.

Kelly leaned over to Colette and nudged her.

"See that guy in the blue jeans and denim jacket?" Kelly whispered. "He's sitting by himself at the table next to the wall."

Colette smiled a little and nodded. "Yeah. That's Miles Perrin."

"Miles? He was the guy in the park on Saturday. What's he like?"

Colette didn't answer right away. "Well, he's—he's kind of spooky. I really don't know much about him. He's a senior. He's really good-looking, as you can see for yourself—"

"Yeah."

"But there's something kind of—well, crazy about him, too," Colette said.

"What do you mean?"

"He's been in a lot of trouble, I know that. With the police, I mean."

"What did he do?"

"I don't really know for sure," Colette said. "I'm not sure the cops have been able to make any charges stick. But he's weird. He seems to hang out alone most of the time. The girls he goes with have bad reputations."

"He looks older than the other guys."

"I'm sure he flunked at least once. He doesn't go to class much, I hear."

"He was staring at me."

"Just ignore him. He's bad news."

"Okay." Kelly thought about how Miles had disap-

31

peared so quickly at the park. "I wonder why he was watching me."

Colette grinned. "Probably because of that long, golden hair and those big blue eyes."

"Oh, right."

"Well, just watch," Colette said. "After the guys around here get to know you a little, you'll be beating them off with a stick." She pulled a copy of the school newspaper out of her bookbag. *This* will certainly get guys to notice you." She opened it and pointed to a picture of three students standing on the school's front steps.

Kelly smiled. "The 'New Students' article. That picture was taken about two weeks ago."

"It's a great interview with you, too. But the best part is that picture, you standing in the middle between those two guys." Colette grinned. "A rose between two thorns."

Kelly laughed.

"And I didn't know you were interested in music. It says you won several piano competitions in your hometown before you came here."

"Yeah."

"That's *terrific!* You should join the school jazz band. They've won some state contests. They're really great."

"The music I play is mostly classical," Kelly said.

"It'd be a chance to meet guys," said Colette. "The jazz band is about ninety-percent male."

Kelly smiled. "That'd be nice." Her smile faded. "I wish I could've met Craig."

"I know," Colette said. "You would've liked him. He made work at the Corner Market kind of fun. I'm really going to miss him."

"This sounds like a heartless change of subject, but I've been meaning to ask you about your job," Kelly said. "I need to earn gas money for driving back and forth to school. Do you think the Corner Market is hiring?"

"Well, now that Craig's dead—"

Kelly winced. "Geez, what a horrible way to get a job."

"I know what you mean," said Colette. "But somebody has to be hired to take his place. It might as well be you. I'll talk to Ron at work tonight."

"Thanks, Colette."

Kelly finished the rest of the day at school. She'd kept her ears open, hoping to learn something about Craig that might point to a reason for his death. But all the talk was about what a nice guy he was. He didn't seem to have any enemies at all.

Kelly picked up her chemistry textbook and notebook at her locker and headed out to the student parking area. The lot was crowded with people standing around in groups, waiting for rides, or hurrying to their cars.

Kelly had arrived at school later than usual this morning and had parked in one of the few spaces left, at the far corner. She hurried, waving to Tracy and calling hello to a guy in her English class along the way.

She passed the second to the last row of cars, spotted her car in the corner, and stopped short.

Miles Perrin was leaning against her red station wagon, his right foot bent up behind him, resting on the front wheel.

He was apparently waiting for her.

She started walking again, consciously keeping her pace steady and purposeful so that he wouldn't guess that seeing him had suddenly made her nervous.

Why should she be nervous, anyway? Just because he turned up at the park on Saturday and stared at her? Or because he caught her eye in the cafeteria today?

Or was it because he was *good-looking* and *spooky,* to use Colette's words?

The girls he goes with have bad reputations, Colette had said. But that didn't mean she couldn't talk to him and find out what he wanted.

Kelly took a deep breath and kept walking. She walked right up to the station wagon, unlocked the passenger door next to Miles, and tossed her chemistry book inside.

"Hi," she said shortly and slammed the door shut.

"Hi," he said. He didn't move from his position against her car. "I read about you in the school paper. You don't look like a musician."

Kelly's heart lurched in her chest, but she tried hard not to let the expression on her face give away her feelings.

"Oh, really? What does a musician look like?"

Miles shrugged. "I don't know. Just not like you."

"Sorry to disappoint you."

He smiled a little and shrugged. "Who says I'm disappointed?"

"I have to get going." Kelly moved past him and around to the driver's side of the car. She could feel Miles's eyes on her, and she felt better with the car standing between them.

"You aren't afraid of me, are you, Kelly?"

Kelly was startled by his directness. She stared hard at him, her heart hammering in her chest.

"Why would I be afraid of you?"

Miles refused to look away and returned the stare. "Some people are."

"Why?"

Miles surprised her by laughing. "I don't know the answer to that question. I really don't."

34

She opened the car door. "I really *do* have to go."

Miles raised his hands as if surrendering to the police.

"Sure."

Kelly got in the car, started up the motor, and without even glancing at Miles again, pulled out of the parking space and out onto the street.

She was more than a mile away before her heart stopped beating so hard.

She *was* frightened, but it wasn't because Miles had a bad reputation, or that he'd been in trouble with the police, or that he was unusually good-looking.

There was a more serious reason for her clammy palms, her shortness of breath, and her thumping heart. It was because when Miles Perrin spoke, Kelly recognized his voice.

He was the man who had hidden in the shadows on Friday night. The man who had spoken to her from behind the monument in the graveyard.

The last person to see Craig Harris alive.

Chapter 5

Kelly had a hard time concentrating on her chemistry homework that night. She sat in her bedroom at the old rolltop desk that Grandad had refinished for her. She was surrounded with lovely antiques, including the canopied bed that she loved so much and the old nightstand that her mother had used when she was a little girl.

Kelly leaned over her schoolwork, resting her elbows on either side of her textbook. The words and numbers blurred and faded on the page in front of her. Replacing them in her mind were images of Craig lying in the ditch and the sound of Miles's deep voice from behind the monument.

" '*He's dead, isn't he?*' " Miles had said to her.

Why did he say that? Did he think Craig was already dead? Or had he seen Craig arrive at the graveyard, perfectly healthy? Was he planning to kill him later, so he decided to let Kelly think Craig was already dead?

She was sure it had been Miles's voice she'd heard from behind the monument. His voice was low, more like a man in his twenties or even thirties. It was distinctive too, the way he slurred his words a little, not as if he were drunk, but just enunciating lazily. His voice also had a soft quality, not what you'd expect from a murderer.

But murderers in real life weren't like the fictional killers in movies and books, were they? The bad guys in films usually had scarred faces, bad teeth, broken noses, and tattoos on their hairy chests and arms.

Miles didn't fit into the killer stereotype at all. He did look rough with his torn jeans and dark, shaggy hair. But his nose was straight, his skin was clear, and his teeth were straight and white.

But it was his eyes that looked least like someone who would murder in cold blood. Miles's eyes were a dark, soft brown. They were troubled eyes, brooding eyes, but not the steely eyes of a killer.

Weren't the eyes supposed to be windows to the soul?

Still, Kelly had seen a real serial killer on the news once who looked like a good-humored, friendly businessman. Nobody would have suspected that his heart and soul were filled with rage and violence.

Colette had said that Miles had a bad reputation. She'd said that he had been in trouble with the police. But for doing what? She wished she knew.

Miles had asked her if she was afraid of him. Was he suggesting that Kelly *should* be afraid? He'd told her that some people are scared of him. Was he warning her?

Colette had called him spooky. That was a good word for Miles, Kelly thought. He *was* kind of spooky.

But was he a murderer?

Kelly sighed and fingered a pencil on her desk. She knew she should go to the police now that she knew who had spoken to her from behind the monument. Her information would probably make Miles a major suspect in their investigation.

She thought of Craig Harris, the nice guy whom everyone liked so much. Shouldn't his death be thoroughly investigated? Kelly knew the answer to that question. *Of course,* and the police should have every bit of information possible.

So would she go to the authorities?

She thought about Alice, Tracy, and Colette. If she talked to the police, she'd drag all of them into it, too. They'd be angry, especially Alice and Tracy, but didn't they deserve that? If they hadn't insisted on playing such an immature trick on her, maybe none of this would have happened. Maybe Craig would still be alive.

But she had promised them she'd wait a week. Those seven days were up this weekend. She guessed she could wait that long.

Maybe by then the police will have caught the murderer, Kelly thought. Then she wouldn't have to be the person to point the finger of suspicion at Miles. Even though she wanted the murderer caught and punished, she didn't want to be responsible for informing the police about Miles. After all, what if she was wrong? There were lots of people who had similar voices. What if he was *innocent?*

So I've decided, she thought. I'll wait. I won't go to the police. At least not yet. At least not until the end of the week. A lot can happen in four days.

"Ron said to come in for an interview tonight," said Colette at lunch the next day. "I gave you a big buildup, and he's definitely interested in talking to you."

The girls had sat down at the end of the table with their usual crowd: Alice, Tracy, and several others from the junior and senior classes.

Kelly smiled. "You didn't tell any lies about me, did you?"

"Of course not! But I showed him the article about you from the school paper."

"Thanks, Colette. I really appreciate it."

"Don't mention it." Colette looked up from her spaghetti and lowered her voice. "Don't look now, but Miles Perrin is staring at you again."

Kelly nodded. She had noticed that he was watching her from his table next to the wall.

"Say, what's going on, anyway?" Colette said. "I saw him talking to you after school in the parking lot yesterday. Is he bothering you or something?"

"Not really," Kelly said. "He just showed up."

Kelly hadn't decided whether to tell Colette that Miles was the guy who had spoken to her from behind the monument. She liked Colette, but she hadn't known her long and wasn't sure exactly where her loyalties were. Colette was a friend of Alice's, and Kelly knew she couldn't trust Alice. Kelly didn't want the information about Miles spread all over school. Not yet, anyway.

"So what did Miles want?"

"I'm not sure," Kelly said truthfully. "I didn't give him a chance to talk very long."

"Good. I told you he was bad news."

"I remember."

"I think he's a little nuts," said Colette, stabbing at a meatball with her fork. "He's always alone. You know, when you hear about a killer on the news and the next-door neighbor is interviewed and says 'The guy always kept to himself'? That's how I think of Miles. Like that quiet guy, filled with violence just ready to explode."

"Really?"

"Yeah. He kind of scares me." Colette glanced up

39

at the clock. "Come on, let's go. I have to get to my history class early. Will you walk with me?"

"Sure. I'll stop by my locker before the crowd rushes in."

The girls picked up their trays and took them back to the window where one of the cooks collected them. Then they headed out the cafeteria door.

Out of the corner of her eye, Kelly saw someone following them.

"Kelly."

Kelly turned to see Miles right behind her. Her heart began to beat harder.

"Can I talk to you a minute?"

Kelly opened her mouth to speak, but Colette jumped in first.

"Kelly and I have to see our history teacher now." It was a lie, of course. Colette's eyes were wide and wary.

"No, that's okay," Kelly said softly to Colette. "I'll see Mr. Williams later."

Colette gave Kelly a hard, disapproving stare.

"I'll talk to Miles," Kelly whispered, "and catch up with you in a minute."

At least he wanted to talk to her inside the school with hundreds of people just around the corner in the cafeteria, she thought. Better that than out in the parking lot. Or somewhere more isolated.

Colette paused a moment, then reluctantly said, "Okay," and headed down the hall.

Kelly turned to Miles. Her fingers began to tremble a little, so she held on to her math book with both hands.

"She's one of those people I told you about," Miles said in his low, soft voice.

"Colette? What do you mean?"

"She's afraid of me." He watched Colette as she walked away from them down the hall.

Kelly swallowed hard. "Should she be?"

Miles's gaze returned to Kelly. "No."

"What do you want, Miles?"

He shrugged. "Just wanted to talk. You mind?" He leaned against the locker behind him.

"No," Kelly said carefully. "What do you want to talk about?"

Miles stared off down the hallway in the direction Colette had gone.

"You like those girls?"

"Colette?"

"Yeah. And the rest. The ones you eat with."

"Well," Kelly said. "I don't know them very well yet. But they were the first friends I met here."

His expression told her nothing.

"Why did you ask about them?"

Miles didn't answer the question.

"You hear about the murder last weekend?"

She took a calming breath. "Yes," she said slowly. "It was terrible. Did you know Craig?"

"Not very well."

Kelly saw something in Miles's eyes that she didn't understand. She didn't know whether it was fear or anger, but he was upset and trying very hard to stay cool.

"Kelly, I have to talk to you." He clenched and unclenched his fist.

"We *are* talking, Miles."

"I mean, alone," Miles said. He took a step toward her. "After school. I'll meet you at your car. We can go somewhere."

Kelly stiffened and took one backward step. "No. If you want to talk, we can stay here at school.

41

Maybe the media center. Nobody's there at the end of the day."

Miles's dark eyes met hers and hung on. "You're afraid of me, aren't you?"

"Of course not." She'd said it too quickly.

"I won't hurt you, Kelly."

She drew in a breath. "I know that."

He continued to stare hard at her. Then he held up his hands. "Okay, I'll meet you in the media center after school."

"Okay."

"In the back, near the far wall."

"Okay."

Miles seemed to relax a little. "I'll see you then."

"See you."

Miles nodded, backed away a little, then turned and strode off down the hall.

Chapter 6

On shaky legs, Kelly approached the media center after school. She'd hardly been able to focus on her classes all afternoon. Her impending meeting with Miles loomed up in her mind and crowded out most every other thought.

She wondered what he needed to say that was so important. And she especially wondered if Miles *was* the guy behind the monument the other night, did he know she had recognized his voice from the graveyard, and if so, what would he do?

She entered the media center, a pleasant, brightly lit space with dark red carpeting and simulated wood bookshelves lining the walls. Tables and study carrels, now empty, were scattered around the large study area in the middle. A central stairway, leading up to more carrels and four discussion rooms, wound its way up to the second floor. Mrs. Harrick, the media specialist and the only other person in the media center, bent over some work at the circulation island and didn't even look up when Kelly walked past her.

Kelly walked directly to the back where she'd agreed to meet Miles, glad that she'd insisted on meeting him here. During the afternoon, the skies had clouded over and turned angry shades of gray and black. The windows along one side of the media center were spattered with rain and the blackness beyond looked more like night than three-thirty in the afternoon. Kelly felt safer inside and was glad for the brightness of the fluorescent lights that burned above the translucent ceiling tiles.

Miles was waiting for her at the back among the bookshelves. He was leaning against the wall.

He nodded to her and then turned his head slightly to gaze at something over her shoulder.

"Come here," he said, pushing off the wall.

He led her to the bottom of the circular metal staircase and stopped. He jerked his chin at it. "Let's go up there."

"Why can't we talk here?"

Miles glanced over at the media specialist. "Upstairs is more private. This talk is between you and me."

Kelly hesitated a moment, decided upstairs should be safe enough, then nodded and climbed the stairs with Miles right behind.

The second floor of the media center was deserted. Study carrels lined the wall to the right side just below long horizontal windows with the dark, troubled sky beyond. A row of glassed-in discussion rooms was on the left.

Miles led Kelly to the farthest discussion room, a cubicle large enough to accommodate a table and chairs for six people. He opened the door in the glassed wall and walked inside. He didn't turn on the light, but turned to face Kelly. She hung back in the doorway.

"Anyone can see us inside," Miles said. "You're safe, Kelly."

"So turn on the light."

44

"I don't want to draw attention to us. I don't want to be interrupted."

Her heart pounding, she walked inside.

Miles closed the door. Now anyone passing the room could see them dimly, but not hear their conversation. Miles nodded to the nearest chair and she sat down. He took his place at the end of the table next to her.

Miles spread his hands on the table and stared at them a moment. He looked agitated, Kelly thought. His breathing was irregular, and from the indirect light shining from the study area beyond the glass wall, she saw the fingers twitch on his right hand. He picked up his hands quickly, self-consciously, and shoved them under the table.

Miles looked up at Kelly. "You were at the graveyard on Friday night, weren't you?"

Kelly was awestruck by his directness.

"Yes, I was."

Why lie? He already knew the truth.

"So were you," she added.

"Yeah. Why were you there?"

"I could ask you the same question."

Careful. Something deep in Kelly's mind warned her not to push him too far, not to make him angry. She didn't know what he might be capable of doing.

"Yeah, you could ask me the same question," Miles said, leaning back in his chair, staring at Kelly. "I'll tell you why I was there. But you tell me first."

Kelly returned his stare and wondered if she would hear the truth from Miles. She didn't know what he'd say, but she was suddenly very curious to hear it.

"I went to the graveyard with Alice, Tracy, and Colette," she said.

Miles's eyes narrowed, but he didn't speak.

"It was kind of an initiation. I didn't know it, but

they'd gotten Craig to agree to play dead in the ditch."

"Why?"

"To scare me."

"Sounds like something they'd do."

"They're nice," Kelly protested. "At least, Colette—"

"They're all the same," Miles said, his voice suddenly hostile.

Kelly now wished she hadn't told him what had happened. He seemed to be the sort of person who would get even with anyone who angered him.

"They scared you, all right," Miles said. "I could tell that." He leaned forward and rested his arms on the table. "Did you tell them what you saw in the ditch?"

"Miles, I don't see any reason to talk about this—" Kelly was worried now for the safety of her friends.

"Answer me, Kelly. Did you tell them about seeing the body in the ditch?"

Kelly scooted her chair back and stood up. "I don't want to talk anymore—"

Miles shoved his chair back so violently that it banged hard against the steel beam in the middle of the glass wall, and he slammed his fist on the table. *"The hell we* won't *talk about it!"*

She rushed for the door, but he reached out and grabbed her around the waist.

Kelly gasped. "Let go of me!"

He immediately released her. He took a deep breath, and sank back into his chair. Kelly could see that he was trying to collect himself, trying to get back in control.

After a moment, he looked up at her. "Sit down." His voice was soft. "I'm sorry." She didn't move. "Please sit down. It won't happen again."

Kelly didn't want to stay, but something kept her from leaving. It was Miles. He looked so miserable, so sad. He seemed genuinely sorry that he'd lost his temper.

Slowly, she sat down, and after a pause, she said, "Your turn."

Miles nodded and stared at the table a moment. "You ever have a good friend? I mean, someone who's more like family than the people you're related to?"

"Yes."

What did this have to do with why he was in the graveyard? Kelly wondered. She didn't speak, though. Her heart was hammering from his outburst, and she didn't want to provoke him again.

Why did she ever agree to meet him?

"I had a friend like that," he said. "Daryl Miller. He was killed last year in a hit-and-run accident."

"I heard about that," Kelly said. "I'm sorry."

"Daryl was—" his voice broke off and he cleared his throat. He was silent a moment.

"You must have really cared about him," she said.

Miles cleared his throat again. "On Friday night, I got a call from Craig Harris. He said he knew something about the accident that killed Daryl. He said there was something he had to do first, but that I should meet him at the edge of the graveyard on Brown Street at midnight.

"I got there early and heard voices—girls' voices—so I walked into the graveyard to see what was going on. It was dark, but there was a full moon that night—"

"You watched us from behind that lilac bush," Kelly said.

"I watched you and those *friends* of yours for a while," he said, emphasizing the word with obvious

47

derision. "I didn't want to hang around them, so I wandered farther into the graveyard. And I found Craig in the ditch. I guess he was playing dead, but I didn't know it at the time. I thought he was *really* dead. And then you came along."

"I thought he was dead, too."

"Maybe he *was.*"

"No," Kelly said. "The paper said his throat was slashed, but when I saw him, the 'blood' I saw was ketchup and was splattered all over the front of his shirt. There wasn't any on his neck or face."

"So you went screaming back to your friends."

"What would you expect me to do?" Kelly said, irritated that Miles would paint a picture of her running like a scared child. "I saw what I thought was a dead body and then I heard this mysterious voice from behind the monument—"

"Did you think I was the murderer?"

"Of course." Kelly opened her mouth to say something else, then closed it. Finally, looking him directly in the eye, she spoke. "Were you?"

"No!" Miles leaned in and his eyes flashed with anger. "I *told* you what happened. Don't you believe me?"

"It—I guess it sounds reasonable," she said. "What happened then? Did Craig get up and walk away?"

Miles let out a deep breath. "I don't know."

"What do you mean, weren't you there?"

"No." He folded his arms across his chest and sank a little into his chair. Then he looked up at Kelly and said it. "I ran, too."

"You ran away?"

Kelly saw him flush, even in the dim light. "You think this is easy for me to say? I ran when you screamed."

"Why?"

"Because I knew you'd bring those girls back with you. Then the cops would come."

"So?"

"So if I stayed there, they'd think that *I* killed Craig."

"You?"

"*You* thought it! And you didn't know anything about me."

"But if you were innocent—"

"What planet are you from, Kelly?" he said scornfully. "I haven't exactly been a Boy Scout, okay? They would've thought I'd killed him, no matter what I told them, no matter what the truth was."

Colette's comment about Miles came back to Kelly then, about him having been in trouble with the police. That trouble must have been pretty bad, or Miles wouldn't be so sure the police would blame him for Craig's murder.

"You didn't see him leave the graveyard?" Kelly asked.

"I told you I didn't."

"So you have no idea who killed Craig."

"No, I don't." Miles drummed his fingers on the table. "So what do we do now?"

"What do you mean?"

"Are you going to the police?" Miles asked.

"I think that'd be a good idea."

"No." Miles stood up and turned to stare out the glass wall, bracing himself with his hands on the metal support beam. Kelly realized he was blocking the only way out of the small room. "You can't go to the cops."

"I have to," Kelly said softly. "You come with me. We'll tell them the story together."

"No, Kelly."

She could hear the anger in his voice again, and her stomach tightened.

He turned and leaned over the table to her. His eyes flashed and his mouth was set in a tight, pale line.

"Don't go to the police. If you do," he paused a moment before finishing, "you'll be sorry."

Kelly stared at him. "Are you threatening me, Miles?"

"Don't go to the police," he repeated. "Promise me you won't go."

"I can't promise—"

"Tell me, Kelly," Miles said. "Tell me you won't talk to the cops."

Kelly didn't answer.

"I know your word is good," Miles said. "That's the kind of person you are." His right eye twitched. "Say you won't go."

"Don't you want Craig's murderer found?"

"Of course I do!" Miles said, leaning in, his eyes fearful. "But we can work on this thing together. Craig must have been killed because he was about to tell me about Daryl's hit-and-run. Don't you see? It has to be connected! We can find out who killed him. Then when we have evidence, we can go to the cops with it."

"You think we can solve a case of *murder?*" Kelly was incredulous. "Just the two of us?"

"Yeah, together. You're really smart, Kelly. About people, I mean. I knew that the first time I talked to you."

Kelly didn't know what to say. Miles's threat that she'd "be sorry" if she talked to the police still rang in her ears. Would he hurt her if she didn't agree to do what he wanted?

Her first wish was to get out of this room. All she

had to do was promise Miles she wouldn't talk to the police. That was easy enough.

But he trusted her. *I know your word is good,* he'd said. Could she betray him after promising?

But she had to get out of here first. She'd worry about the rest later.

"I promise," she said. "I won't talk to the police. Yet."

"Never," he said. "Not until we can prove who killed Craig."

Kelly took a deep breath. "Okay." She'd try to reason with him later.

"You promise?"

"Yes, I promise."

Miles sank with relief into his chair. "Good. Thank you, Kelly. Thank you."

Chapter 7

"Ready for your first night?" Colette asked. She handed Kelly a red smock. *Corner Market* was stitched over the right breast pocket.

"I think so," Kelly said. She put the smock on over her denim skirt and print cotton blouse.

Last evening, Kelly had interviewed for the job at the Corner Market. Ron, the manager, was obviously impressed with her, and offered her the position. Because of Craig's sudden death, he needed her to start right away. So here she was, the following night, starting her job as a cashier in the small grocery store.

The Corner Market stood on a commercial street at the edge of a residential neighborhood. As its name implied, it was located on the corner at one end of a strip mall. Next door was a drug store, and farther over were several other small retail outlets: a dress shop, a hair salon, and a video rental store. At the far end was a small branch bank.

The inside of the store was pleasant, clean, and brightly lit. Employees were working behind the cash registers, sacking, and pushing carts of groceries out to the parking lot for customers.

"Now don't get upset if Trudy throws too many

things at you all at once," Colette said. "She trained me, and I was absolutely overwhelmed at all the stuff I had to learn!"

"How long till you caught on to everything?"

"Oh, I *still* have to ask Trudy questions occasionally."

"And you've been working here for a year?"

Colette grinned. "Yeah. But the things you do every day you'll feel comfortable with by—oh, maybe by the end of the week. Or next."

"You like the people who work here?"

"Mostly. You already know Alice Roe. She's over at register four."

Kelly turned to see the small blonde ringing up items for an elderly woman and her husband.

She was disappointed that Alice was here tonight. Alice wasn't someone with whom she wanted to spend any more time than necessary.

"Almost everyone here has become a friend." Colette lowered her voice. "Except for Jeremy Watts, who's a total jerk."

"Who's Jeremy Watts?"

Colette nodded toward a big guy with light brown hair who was sacking groceries. "He's a senior. Maybe you've seen him around at school."

"No, I haven't." Kelly was about to ask Colette why she disliked Jeremy so much, when Ron, the manager, approached.

"Hi, Kelly." Ron Ralston was probably in his midforties, Kelly thought. He was tall and slender and wore slacks and a dress shirt and tie. He smiled. "Ready to go?"

"I think so," Kelly said, smiling. "I'm a little nervous about all I have to learn."

"You'll be fine. Trudy'll be training you, and she

does a good job. Come on over here, and I'll introduce you."

Ron led her to the last checkout lane, where a woman stood bent over some papers at a closed register.

"Trudy, this is Kelly McLees. She's our new cashier."

Trudy stood up and offered her hand. She looked in her early thirties, with dark, curly hair and a big, infectious grin.

"Hi, Kelly, glad to meet you."

"Hi."

"Let's get to work, okay?"

"Sure."

Kelly spent the next hour and a half with Trudy at the cash register learning and practicing how to sack groceries, how to "sign on" to the cash register using her personal identification number, how to ring up a sale using the scanner, and how to tender out the order to close the sale, punching up the correct buttons on the register when the customer uses a check, cash, or credit card.

"Wow," Kelly said, shaking her head. "I knew I'd have a lot to learn, but I never thought it'd be *this* much!"

Trudy grinned. "This is just the beginning. We haven't touched on what to do when a customer pays with food stamps or buys a Lotto ticket, or uses discount coupons."

"My gosh."

"Or how to ring up a sale using the produce scale, or take markdown items, or—"

"Who's the new babe?"

The voice surprised Kelly. She turned to see Jeremy Watts standing behind her. He was smiling, but it wasn't a friendly smile. It was more of a sneer. He looked her up and down.

"Goldilocks? That your name? The girl with the long, golden hair?"

"No," Kelly said, self-consciously tucking a strand of hair behind her ear. "My name's Kelly."

"This is Kelly McLees," Trudy said. "She's just starting tonight. She's taking Craig's place."

"Jumping in to grab the spoils, eh? One person's murder is another person's gain, I guess."

"Jeremy, don't you have a break to go on, or something?" Trudy said crossly.

Jeremy's sneer faded. His cheeks colored a little, but if he was embarrassed, his expression didn't give him away. "Yeah. I need a cigarette."

"Good. Get lost then. And do your smoking outside."

Jeremy's jaw tightened, but he forced an insincere smile at Kelly. "'Bye, Goldilocks."

He strode off down the aisle toward the back of the store.

Trudy rolled her eyes. "What an—" She stopped herself. "I was about to say something really nasty."

"Go ahead," Kelly said. "I'll probably agree with you."

"He's really a horrid person, but Ron won't fire him because he's a pretty good worker. The older women customers think he's wonderful."

"You're kidding."

"No. For some reason, he's nice when he's around them. Everyone who works here knows it's an act, but the customers don't know that, and they love him." She shrugged. "Go figure." She stared off toward the back. "Sorry for that crack about Craig."

This time Kelly shrugged. "That's okay. Colette told me that Craig had worked here."

"Yeah. A really nice guy. Everybody liked him."

"It's hard to believe that a murder could happen here in Spencer Point. It seems like such a peaceful town."

Kelly wasn't just making idle conversation. She hoped she might learn more about Craig. Maybe something that would help her figure out who murdered him.

After her talk with Miles, she'd decided to give herself another deadline. Since she'd promised Miles she wouldn't go to the police yet, she'd try to find out all she could about Craig. If she hadn't learned anything by next week at this time, she'd go to the police with or without Miles.

She knew Miles would be furious when he learned what she was going to do, but she didn't allow herself to think about that, about his threat. Instead, she wanted to concentrate on learning all she could about Craig.

"This really *is* a peaceful town most of the time," Trudy was saying. "But Craig's murder is the second strange death we've had in two years."

"I heard about the hit-and-run," Kelly said. "Daryl—wasn't that the guy's name?"

"Yes. He was a little weird, I guess, but he was nice enough. He worked here, too, you know."

This news startled Kelly. "No. No, I didn't know that."

"Yes. He and Craig were as different as night and day, but they were both good workers."

Both Craig and Daryl worked here together. Could there be a connection between their deaths and their jobs at the Corner Market?

"How were they different?"

"Oh, Craig was the kid next door. He was handsome, got good grades, came from a nice family—the kind of guy you'd bring home to meet your parents. Daryl, on the other hand, wasn't particularly good-looking, his family had lots of problems, and I think he was a pretty uninterested student."

"It's strange that two guys were killed in Spencer Point and both worked here."

"Yes," said Trudy, tucking a pencil behind her ear. "I've thought about that myself. I think the police have, too. They've been around here asking lots of questions. But for the life of me, I can't imagine how the two killings might be connected."

"Did Craig and Daryl work here at the same time?"

"Yes, there was some overlap," Trudy said. "Daryl started working here two years ago. Craig was hired about three months before Daryl was killed. I wondered that myself, and looked it up even before the homicide detective asked me about it."

"You think the police suspect a connection?"

"I don't know. They've asked so many questions about everything, it's hard to tell."

"Kelly," Ron called out from the manager's booth near the door. "We're getting pretty busy here. Could you help sack and carry-out at register four?"

"Sure," Kelly said. She looked at Trudy. "I hope I remember what you told me about sacking."

"Just make sure to square out the bottom of the sack," Trudy said. "Small boxes to the outside, heavy stuff in the middle. And use the sack size that fits the order."

"Right."

Kelly hurried to register four, where Alice was working.

"Hi, Alice."

"Hi," Alice answered over her shoulder. "Mrs.

Granville needs a carry-out. I already sacked it for you."

"Okay." Kelly smiled at Mrs. Granville, a large matronly woman wearing several bracelets on each wrist that clanked together noisily.

Mrs. Granville looked past Kelly and then over her shoulder.

"Is Jeremy here tonight?" she asked.

"He's on break," Alice said.

"Oh," she said. She looked disappointed.

Kelly had a hard time keeping a straight face. Jeremy really must put on a phony personality for the ladies! Surely if Mrs. Granville knew the *real* Jeremy—

"My car's parked on the far side of the lot," Mrs. Granville said, marching toward the door.

Kelly wheeled the grocery cart outside, following Mrs. Granville, and loaded the sacks into the trunk of her Mercedes.

"Thank you, dear," said Mrs. Granville.

"You're welcome. Have a nice evening."

Kelly walked back inside, pushing the grocery cart.

The store was very busy, and Kelly worked constantly at Alice's register for the next hour, sacking and carrying out groceries.

When Jeremy returned from his break, he sacked at the next register, number three, where Colette was working as cashier.

"Mrs. Granville asked for you," Alice said to Jeremy between customers.

Jeremy laughed. "She's got a crush on me. What can I say, I'm irresistible."

"You're an arrogant jerk, that's what you are," Alice murmured, turning away.

"What? Did you say something to me?"

By the sarcasm in his voice, Kelly knew Jeremy had heard every word.

Alice turned back to Jeremy, put a hand on her hip, and looked at him straight in the eye. "I said you're an arrogant jerk."

Jeremy smirked. "Alice, could it be that you're jealous of Mrs. Granville?"

"Of that old bag? You've got to be kidding."

Just then a woman approached Colette's cash register. She was slim and attractive, probably in her early forties with dyed potato-chip-colored hair. She wore an expensive and colorful jogging outfit and running shoes.

"Hi, Mrs. Hawkins," Colette said.

"Hello," she said to Colette, then turned a megawatt smile on Jeremy. "Hi, Jeremy."

"Well, if it isn't my favorite customer," Jeremy said. Kelly could almost feel the ooze in his well-oiled line.

"Did you get your car fixed?"

"Yes, ma'am. Turned out I needed a new alternator. Damn, those're expensive. Excuse my French."

Mrs. Hawkins beamed. "You're excused. *This* time."

An elderly woman stopped at Alice's register and started, with great difficulty, to pull a large sack of potatoes out of her cart.

"I'll get that for you," Kelly said.

The old woman hadn't bought much, but Kelly used two sacks for her purchases. Elderly people, Trudy had said, would rather make extra trips to the house from their car to unload groceries than have to carry a smaller number of heavy loads.

The woman paid for her purchases with cash and Kelly wheeled the cart out to the parking lot.

"It's the brown Chevy," the woman said, pointing.

Jeremy and Mrs. Hawkins were chatting next to her white BMW, which was parked next to the brown Chevy. There was no cart there, so Jeremy must have carried the bags out for her.

Kelly stopped her cart in back of the Chevy and the old woman opened her trunk.

"Then we're gong to London," Mrs. Hawkins was saying. "Richard and I have been there before, but there's so much we missed the first time."

Kelly loaded the groceries into the Chevy. She glanced sideways at Jeremy. He stood with his arms folded, and leaning against Mrs. Hawkins's car.

"Sounds great," Jeremy said enthusiastically. "When're you leaving?"

"Tomorrow," Mrs. Hawkins said, laughing. "I have so much to do! Before a month-long trip, there are so many details to take care of!"

"Just like your daughter's wedding last summer," Jeremy said.

"No, nothing could be *that* bad!" Mrs. Hawkins said, her laughter louder this time.

"Well, have a terrific time," Jeremy said.

"I'll send you a postcard," said Mrs. Hawkins.

"You do that."

Mrs. Hawkins waved and walked around to the driver's door, unlocked it, got in, and started the engine.

Jeremy slammed the trunk closed and glanced, for the first time, over at Kelly. She quickly looked away, back at the elderly woman standing next to her.

Kelly closed the truck of the woman's car. "Have a nice evening," she said.

"Thank you."

Kelly wheeled her cart toward the store while both cars drove away.

"Hey, Goldilocks."

Kelly slowed and turned toward Jeremy.

"Were you staring at me?"

"No."

"Yes, you were," he said. He didn't smile, didn't even sneer. "What's so fascinating about me, anyway?"

"Nothing, Jeremy." She continued to wheel the cart toward the store, wishing the old woman had parked in any other spot.

Jeremy caught up with her at the store's entrance and put an arm around her shoulder. "Well, you know what?" he said.

"What?" She didn't like Jeremy touching her.

"What I do is none of your business. You got that, babe?"

Kelly sighed and wriggled away. "Sure, Jeremy," she said, pretending to be bored with this exchange.

"Yeah, well, you remember that."

He strode on into the store ahead of her.

Chapter 8

Kelly was busy the next several days, going to school, getting her homework done, then working through the evenings at the Corner Market.

She hadn't seen Miles since their talk in the media center. She wondered if he had classes at opposite ends of the building or if he just wasn't coming to school.

The Corner Market job was getting easier as she became more acquainted with the intricacies of a grocery cashier's duties. In fact, she was beginning to enjoy the time between six and ten every night. She had even learned the names of several of the regular customers that Trudy pointed out so she could call them by name the next time they came in. This was an important requirement of all the store employees.

She enjoyed working with Ron, Trudy, and Colette, but she tried to steer clear of Alice and especially Jeremy whenever possible. Alice and Jeremy continued to trade insults and Jeremy continued to be extravagantly polite to the older women customers, who lapped up his attention with apparent delight.

After work on Saturday night, she grabbed her jacket, said good-bye to Colette and Trudy, and walked out to her car.

It was ten o'clock and the parking lot was dark and nearly deserted, holding only the cars of the few employees still inside the store. The air was chilly and even in her light woolen jacket, Kelly shivered as she fumbled for the key in her purse.

"Kelly."

At first she didn't see him. The voice came from the far edge of the parking lot. She squinted into the darkness, wishing her eyes would adjust to the dim light after being under fluorescent all evening.

A moment later the dark figure came into view. He sat on a motorcycle in the deep shadows of a large elm tree. Kelly recognized Miles and felt her heart quicken. She really wasn't afraid of him, but he was so unpredictable, he made her nervous.

"Come here."

Kelly walked across the lot and stopped in front of his motorcycle.

"Hi, Miles."

His hair was messed up from riding in the wind. He wore a dark leather jacket, gloves, jeans, and boots.

"Hi, yourself. I see you got a job."

"Yeah."

"Daryl worked here, you know," Miles said.

"I know. So did Craig."

"That right?" Miles was silent a moment. "That's quite a coincidence."

"I don't know if there's a connection or not."

"So you're playing detective without me?" Miles gazed at her curiously.

"I got a job. I needed gas money for my car."

"Learn anything useful?"

Kelly smiled. "You mean like how to ring up the sale of a lottery ticket?"

A small grin played at the corner of Miles's mouth.

"Don't be a wiseguy." He scratched his cheek, then folded his arms, and the smile faded. "Like maybe who could've murdered Daryl or Craig."

"No."

"So what do you think of these people you're working with?"

"You mean, do I like them?"

"Yeah."

Kelly shrugged. "Most of them."

Miles looked up over Kelly's shoulder. "Alice Roe works here?"

Kelly turned to see Alice getting into her car across the lot.

"Yes, she does."

"She still your good buddy?"

"She's all right." Kelly didn't feel like agreeing with Miles about Alice.

"You trust these people?"

"Most of them."

"Don't," Miles said seriously. "You can't trust anybody."

"Including you?"

This time Miles grinned widely. "You really are a wiseguy, you know. Who taught you that?"

In spite of her nervousness, Kelly grinned back. "It's my nature, I guess. I can't help it."

"Yeah? Well, you're very cute."

Kelly didn't know what to say to that. She didn't want to encourage Miles to get any closer.

"Thanks," she said finally in a soft voice, staring down at his boots.

"Want to go for a ride?"

"On your motorcycle?"

"No, on my skateboard." Miles laughed. "Of course, on my motorcycle."

"No, I don't think so."

"Why not?"

"It looks scary. And I don't have a helmet."

"Neither do I."

"You should. What if you had an accident?"

Miles laughed again. "You've got to take risks sometimes."

"Not with my life."

"Don't you trust me?"

Kelly smiled. "Not especially. Besides, you just told me not to trust anybody."

"What do I have to do to win you over, Kelly?"

Kelly shrugged and continued to smile a little, but didn't answer.

"You name it."

"How come I never see you around school?" Kelly asked.

"You changed the subject."

"Don't you go to class?"

"I'm around."

"That's not an answer."

"I'm at school," Miles said, irritation coloring his voice. "Okay?"

"Okay," Kelly said. She was too tired to deal with an outburst of temper tonight. She took a step backward. "Well, I'd better be getting home."

"You'll tell me if you find out something, won't you?"

"About Craig's murder?"

Miles nodded. "Or Daryl's."

"Yes, I'll tell you."

"Good," Miles said. "I wouldn't want you to go to the police."

"I thought that was the whole idea," Kelly said. "To learn something about the murders and then go to the police with the information."

"That depends on what the information is."

65

A thought was nudging at Kelly. "Miles, you aren't thinking of doing something *yourself*, are you? I mean, for revenge?"

"We all do what we have to do."

Kelly felt the anger well up in the center of her chest, then spread throughout her body.

"Then don't count on me to help you, Miles. I'm not going to have blood on my hands! Yours or anybody else's. And I'd appreciate it if you'd leave me alone from now on."

She turned and stalked away toward her car.

"Kelly, I didn't mean to make you mad."

She didn't answer, but strode to her car, got in, and drove out of the parking lot.

"Pass the funnypapers, will you, Kelly?" her grandfather said from the kitchen table.

Kelly had just come in from picking up the Sunday morning paper. The rural carrier always left it in the postbox alongside the road.

"Sure." Kelly unfolded the paper and handed her grandfather the comics section. "You want *Parade* magazine, Nana?"

"That would be nice, dear."

Kelly looked through the paper, pulled out the colorful magazine insert, and handed it to her grandmother. Then she wandered into the living room and collapsed on the couch. Lifting her feet to rest on the ottoman, she flipped the paper over to read the front page under the fold line.

A headline caught her eye: "Another Home Burglarized."

She scanned the article and stopped on the name of the homeowners: Mr. and Mrs. Richard Hawkins.

The name was familiar. Then she remembered.

Mrs. Hawkins was the customer she'd seen at the store several days ago.

She went back to the beginning of the article and read the whole thing. Police said thieves gained access to the house on Friday evening by breaking a window in the basement. Among the missing items were a CD/stereo system, two television sets, a microwave oven, and a home computer. A neighbor who was looking after the house while the Hawkins couple was on vacation discovered the break-in and reported it to the police.

The article went on to report that this was the most recent in a series of break-ins in Spencer Point. Most of them centered in the wealthiest part of town, a section called Spellman Heights. All of the residents had been away on vacation when their homes were burglarized.

Kelly lowered the paper into her lap as the memory of—when was it?—Wednesday evening came back to her. It was her first day at work. She was in the parking lot at the store and Mrs. Hawkins was talking to Jeremy, telling him about her planned trip to Europe.

"When are you leaving?" Jeremy had asked.

"Tomorrow. I have so much to do!" she had said, laughing.

Why did Jeremy want to know when she was leaving? Kelly had assumed he was just buttering her up because she was a rich, attractive customer.

But buttering her up for what? What could he get from a woman like Mrs. Hawkins? She certainly wouldn't be interested in a romance with a high school guy.

Besides, that older woman—what was her name? Oh, yes, Mrs. Granville. She had looked for Jeremy, too. And she wasn't young or even particularly attractive. Jeremy couldn't have been interested in her for any reason other than that she was rich.

Was Jeremy becoming friendly with the rich women customers to find out when they would be traveling and away from home? *Could Jeremy be responsible for the rash of break-ins in Spellman Heights?*

Jeremy had been out in the parking lot with Mrs. Hawkins when they had the discussion about her vacation. Did he make sure to hold that conversation outside, away from the other employees, where they wouldn't be overheard?

But they *had* been overheard. And Jeremy knew it. He'd even gone so far as to tell Kelly to mind her own business.

And Kelly had done just that for the rest of the week. She'd avoided Jeremy. She'd taken every opportunity to put distance between them, to keep her eyes and ears focused on other people and activities. She hadn't wanted a run-in with Jeremy. He was just too unpleasant.

Kelly realized all she had was a theory. So what if Jeremy chatted with the rich women customers? So what if they told him about their upcoming trips? Jeremy and the ladies talked about a lot of things. Just yesterday, Kelly had heard Jeremy talking with—what was her name? Mrs. Lodge, that was it. She was telling him about all of her grandchildren. She'd said she has ten! Jeremy had joked with her about the Old Woman and the Shoe, and she had laughingly reminded him that she wasn't old.

Yes, Jeremy was a hypocritical jerk. But that wasn't enough to convince the police that he was responsible for the break-ins.

Kelly tucked her legs up under her on the couch. She decided to keep an eye on Jeremy and listen to

68

his conversations with the wealthy women customers. If she noticed on more occasions—maybe two or three—that a robbery occurred shortly after a customer was in the store talking to Jeremy about a trip, she'd have more to tell the police.

She smiled a little, thinking that she really *had* become a detective, just as Miles had said. Maybe she really *was* up to solving a crime or two.

And that's when the thought came to her. It sprang into her mind fully formed and stood before her, commanding her full attention.

Could Daryl or Craig—or *both*—have discovered a link between the burglaries and Jeremy's curious friendships with the women who shop at the store? Could the boys have been *murdered* because of what they had uncovered?

Kelly began trembling and a shot of adrenaline coursed through her body. Suddenly, her suspicions about Jeremy were taking on horrible new dimensions.

Had she just discovered something that had caused the death of two people?

If she were not careful from here on in, could she be the next victim?

Chapter 9

"He's a jerk, Kelly."

Kelly looked up, startled. She had been watching Jeremy out of the corner of her eye while she worked at cash register number five on Sunday afternoon. He was working with Trudy, sacking groceries across the store at the first register.

Kelly hadn't been aware anyone was watching *her*. She turned to face Alice, who had spoken. It had been a slow day, and there were no customers at any of the registers past the first one.

Alice stared at Kelly, leaning against the counter with her arms folded. She scowled.

"You have a crush on him or something?"

Kelly was aware that Colette, at register four on her other side, had turned around to hear the conversation.

"Are you kidding?" Kelly said.

"No," Alice said. "You keep staring at him all the time."

"He's just—" What would she say? She certainly didn't want to voice any of her suspicions. She had no evidence to back it up. "I can't figure out why he's so mean to everyone except the women who come in here." She smiled. "Do you think he has a split personality?"

"Probably."

"I think he's hoping to get written into their wills," Colette said.

Kelly laughed, relieved that the conversation was taking a lighter tone.

"I mean it!" Colette said, grinning. "He has to have an ulterior motive. Jeremy'd never be nice without having a selfish reason."

"But he's polite to *all* the women customers," Alice pointed out. "Not just the rich ones."

"That's true," Kelly said.

"I can't figure him out," Colette said. "He's really creepy."

"He's a jerk," Alice said. "He loves himself to death. He thinks he's the best-looking, sexiest, most wonderful guy on the face of the earth."

"Yeah," Colette said. "What an ego. Too bad he's so good-looking."

Kelly laughed and turned to the man who had approached her register. She was glad to end the conversation about Jeremy, but alarmed that her attention to him had been so obvious. If Alice had noticed it, maybe Jeremy had, too. She was going to have to be more careful.

Kelly made her way down the crowded hall before lunch on Monday. She saw Jeremy walking toward her, so she turned her head to avoid having to acknowledge him. Since she'd come up with her theory about his possible crimes, just seeing him gave her the creeps.

Even though she was very hungry, she decided to stop at her locker first to get the books and spirals she'd need for her afternoon classes. She'd be on the third floor for the rest of the day.

Kelly's locker was located on the main floor across from the office. She whirled the combination lock and flung the door open.

She stopped short and stared at what she saw.

On the shelf above the coat hook sat a helmet. A motorcycle helmet. A piece of masking tape with the name KELLY written in large, block letters was stuck to it just above the visor.

Kelly smiled. A peace offering from Miles.

She took the helmet down from the shelf and turned it around in her hands. A scrawl inside the helmet just over the ear caught her attention.

TIM PORTER, it said in handwritten ink.

Kelly sighed. Great. Miles had given her a stolen motorcycle helmet. Just what she needed.

She pushed it back onto her shelf, closed the door, and gave the combination lock a quick turn.

That's when she realized that Miles had broken into her locker to leave his surprise present. She always locked her locker. Always.

She shook her head and started down the hall to the cafeteria. Miles was a strange guy, all right. His idea of a special gift was a stolen piece of merchandise delivered after breaking and entering.

Miles was sitting alone in his usual spot near the wall. He'd already picked up his lunch, which sat before him on an orange tray. Kelly walked over and sat down next to him.

"I found the helmet, Miles," she said.

Miles gave her a little smile. "So you going to ride with me now?"

"Miles, I think it was nice that you wanted to give me a present, but don't you think you'd better return it?"

"What do you mean?"

"It says 'Tim Porter' inside. Don't you think he's looking for his helmet?"

The smile on Miles's face faded and a shadow crossed his face. He turned and stared at the wall, his face red with anger, but he didn't say anything.

"Miles? I just feel sorry for the guy. It's a great helmet—"

Miles stood up abruptly. He reached down, and with a sweep of his arm shoved his lunch tray, all of its contents clattering to the floor.

Every head in the cafeteria turned their way as Miles strode across the room and out the door.

Kelly didn't see Miles for the rest of the day. Colette wanted to know what had happened between them to cause Miles to dump his lunch on the floor, but Kelly didn't explain. She realized that Miles thought he was doing something nice for her. He didn't need to have the whole school talking about the stolen helmet.

Kelly just wanted him to leave her alone. His temper outbursts alone were reason enough not to see him. She didn't think he was involved in the murders, but she didn't doubt that he was a thief. The motorcycle helmet was surely not the first thing he'd stolen. Nor was her locker the first place he'd broken into.

After school, she headed out to the student parking area. The lot was crowded this time of the afternoon, and she wound her way around and between the cars. She saw Miles walking to the other side of the lot, and she turned away, not wanting to speak to him.

She looked over where she'd parked her car and was surprised to see it surrounded with students.

"What's going on?" she murmured and picked up her pace.

One of the students, a boy in her P.E. class, looked up and grinned when she got near.

"This your car?" he asked.

"Yeah. What's wrong?"

"You got somebody mad at you?" another guy said.

He pointed to her tire.

"It's slashed."

Kelly rushed to the car and bent down to examine the right front tire. The guy was right. It hadn't just lost air from a nail puncture. The tire had been cut in several places, long slashes with a sharp knife or tool.

"Oh, *no,*" she said. Tires weren't cheap, and it would cost at least her first week's wages to replace this one.

"It wasn't just that one," a girl said. "They're all cut."

"What?"

"Boy, somebody sure is P.O.'ed at you!"

Kelly stood back and looked at her car. The whole automobile was lower by several inches, the tires drooping, and the wheel rims resting on the ground. It was going to take a month's wages to pay for new tires.

She was suddenly consumed with rage that someone would inflict so much damage to her car, so much expensive damage. She kicked at a ruined tire and swore loudly, then paced angrily back and forth.

"Want me to call a tow?" one of the boys asked.

"Yeah, yeah," she said. Her mind was not able to focus very well because it was so filled with fury.

"If you know who did this, you can bring charges against him," said another boy.

74

"I know."

"You know who did it?"

"No, but I have an idea." She thought about Miles's bad temper, about him shoving his lunch on the floor. "I just might bring charges at that."

She surveyed the damage again and nodded. She clutched her car keys so tightly her fingers were mottled with purple and white. "I just might bring those charges."

Chapter 10

Kelly sat in Ron's booth and ran her finger down the listings in the phone book. *Poppen, Porod, Porter.*

There it was: Tim Porter on Avis Drive.

She'd had so much to do after school, arranging for her car to be towed, buying the new tires with money borrowed from her grandfather, and waiting for the tires to be put on her car, she didn't have time to make the call at home.

Kelly had arrived at work a little early, and Ron's booth was deserted, so she found him and asked if she could use his phone. She had decided to call the owner of the motorcycle helmet. She had no intention of mentioning Miles. She only wanted the helmet returned to its rightful owner.

She dialed the number and waited. It was answered after the third ring.

"Hello?" Kelly said. "Is this Tim Porter?"

"Speaking."

"Do you have a motorcycle?"

"Sure do."

"I found a motorcycle helmet yesterday," she said. "It has your name in it. Did you lose it?"

"Uh, no," he said slowly. "My name's in it?"

"Yes. Tim Porter."

"Oh! I remember!" he said. "That must be the helmet I donated to Goodwill a couple of weeks ago. My old one."

Kelly was stunned. "You donated it?"

"Yeah. To Goodwill. You know, they resell stuff secondhand. They probably charged a dollar or two for it."

"Oh." A terrible warmth spread through her body.

"Someone probably bought it and then lost it."

Miles had bought the helmet for her and she'd accused him of stealing it!

"Yes," she said mechanically.

"Thanks for calling, though."

"Sure."

Kelly hung up feeling sick to her stomach. She had done a terrible thing and she felt guilty and very upset.

Miles hadn't even defended himself. Why? He certainly hadn't hidden his anger, but he didn't explain where the helmet had come from, either.

She flipped back a few pages of the phone book.

"Miles Perrin, Perrin," she whispered to herself, scanning the list of names.

There was only one Perrin listed, Frank Perrin.

She dialed the number.

The phone was picked up on the other end.

"Hello." The man's voice was loud.

"Hi," Kelly said. "Is Miles there?"

"No, he ain't! Who's asking?" He sounded angry.

"Uh," Kelly faltered, startled by the man's roughness. "My name is Kelly McLees."

"What do you want with Miles?"

The words were a little slurred, and it was then that Kelly realized the man—was it Miles's father?—was drunk.

"I'll just talk to him at school tomorrow."

"Yeah, you do that."

The phone was slammed down.

Kelly sighed deeply and hung up. Poor Miles. He didn't seem to have an easy life, that was for sure.

And I contributed to that, Kelly thought. *How could I have assumed he stole the helmet?*

She knew if another person in her class had given her something with someone else's name inside, she wouldn't have jumped to conclusions like that.

Miles *did* break into her locker, there was no other way for him to get inside. But he didn't steal the helmet.

Then she wondered: Did he slash her tires?

Could it have been someone else?

Kelly replaced the phone book in the top right-hand drawer of Ron's desk. She sat back in Ron's chair and gazed absentmindedly out the booth door to the cash registers along the front of the store. Jeremy was sacking groceries. He looked up then, right at Kelly. His face didn't change, but something about the way he stared at her made her stiffen.

Maybe it wasn't Miles who slashed her tires. Maybe the tire incident had nothing to do with the helmet.

Maybe it had more to do with burglary.

And murder.

"I saw you talking with Miles after work one night last week," Colette said, tossing a piece of candy in her mouth. She tipped her folding metal chair backward until it touched the cement-block wall behind her.

Colette and Kelly were taking a short break in the employee lounge in the basement of the Corner Market. Colette's break had begun ten minutes earlier than Kelly's, so they had only a few minutes to talk.

The girls sat at a long table that was cluttered with empty soda cans, coffee cups, and discarded candy wrappers. An intercom speaker hung on the wall overhead. Ron sometimes used it to call employees up early when traffic became heavy in the store.

"Yeah," Kelly said, setting down her can of Coke. She hoped Colette wouldn't push too hard or ask too many questions. "He stopped by."

"Miles is interested in you," Colette said. "Isn't he?"

"Oh, I don't know," Kelly said, evasively. "Maybe he's just lonely."

"Well, don't play social worker with him," Colette warned. "You have a soft heart, and he would spot that in a minute and take advantage of you."

Kelly wondered why Colette was so sure Miles was a bad guy. "Do you know him very well?"

"Well, no, but I know his type," Colette said. "He's got a bad rep, I told you that already." She rolled the candy around in her mouth, then tucked it in her cheek. "So what did he want?"

"Miles?"

Colette rolled her eyes and grinned. "Of *course*, Miles! We're talking about him, aren't we?"

"He stopped to say hi, I guess. We didn't talk very long."

Colette cocked her head to one side and stared at Kelly. "Do you attract guys like him?"

"What do you mean?"

"Well, I saw Jeremy staring at you the other day. Miles is spooky and Jeremy is such a jerk, I just wondered if this usually happens to you, that weirdos fall in love with you."

"Jeremy was staring at me?" Adrenaline began pumping through her body. "When was that?"

"Yesterday. He was watching you carry groceries

from inside the glass door. He watched you all the way out, but he hurried back to his register as soon as you started back inside."

Kelly forced a smile she didn't feel. "Well, to answer your question, no, I wouldn't say that I normally have a long line of nut cases trailing along behind me."

"So you think Miles is a nut case, too, huh?"

"Well, no, not really. He seems to have a pretty short fuse. But I don't think he's crazy."

A pair of feet clicked down the wooden stairs behind them and Alice walked over to the table.

"Your break's over, Colette. Ron wants your butt upstairs."

Colette grinned and stood up. "I'll bet he didn't put it that way. Ron's more refined than that."

"You calling me unrefined, Colette?" Alice scowled and pushed her coins into the soda machine.

"Who, me?" Colette laughed and disappeared up the stairs.

"Funny girl," Alice said sourly. She pulled her can of root beer out of the machine and collapsed into the chair nearest Kelly.

There was a minute of silence between them while Alice sat sullenly drinking her soda and Kelly debated with herself about whether to try and talk to Alice about Daryl and Craig. She didn't know whether Alice knew anything that would be of help in solving the murders or whether she would even talk about them. Alice didn't appear to be in a very good mood. In fact, the only time Kelly had seen Alice be anything but grouchy was in the graveyard, when she was quivering with fear of the snake outside the caretaker's cabin.

On the other hand, Kelly didn't see Alice alone very often. Maybe she would offer some information now that she wouldn't be willing to talk about in front of other people. Kelly decided to give it a shot.

"Did you work at the Corner Market when Daryl was here?" Kelly finally asked.

Alice didn't look up. She stared at the shiny metal can in her hand. "Yeah. We started working here about the same time."

"What was he like?"

"Kind of weird."

"In what way?"

"He didn't talk much. Kept to himself. He had bad teeth and crummy clothes."

"That's too bad," Kelly said. "His family must've been poor, and maybe he didn't have much self-confidence."

Alice looked up smugly at Kelly. "You really are a bleeding heart, aren't you?"

"What do you mean?"

"So understanding. Always saying the right things. Always doing the right things."

Kelly decided to ignore Alice's snide remarks and get to the point.

"Do you think there's a connection between Daryl's and Craig's deaths?"

Alice shrugged. "I don't know why there would be. Why? Do *you* think there's a connection?"

"I don't know. I didn't know either of them."

Alice looked at her with a deadpan expression. "But you think it's your duty as a good, moral person to try to uncover the reasons for their deaths."

Kelly forced a smile and lifted her can of soda to her lips. "I'm just naturally curious."

Alice rolled her eyes.

"You aren't still planning to go to the police about our little game in the graveyard, are you?"

"No," said Kelly. "Not yet, anyway."

"What's that supposed to mean?"

"Well, I've decided that our 'game' probably didn't have anything to do with Craig's death."

"Smart girl. I told you that from the beginning."

"Some of us learn slower than others," Kelly said, more to smooth Alice's angry edge than because she believed it about herself. "But it's possible that if the police knew that Craig was in the graveyard late on Friday night, they'd be able to retrace his steps and find out who might have killed him."

"You'd better not get me involved," Alice said.

"You were there, Alice."

"Listen," Alice said, leaning forward. "None of us needs a smear on our reputations. I don't know about you, but I'm applying to some pretty high-powered schools out East. I don't need to get involved in a case of murder I had nothing to do with."

"Didn't you like Craig?"

"Sure, but so what? He's *dead!* I can't do anything for him now!" She glanced at her watch. "Hey, listen, I've got to run to the bank and get some cash at the ATM. If I'm a minute or two late, cover for me, will you? Tell Ron I'm in the can or something."

"Okay."

"Kelly!" Ron's voice sounded from the intercom. "Shave a minute off your break, will you? We're getting busier up here. You can leave a minute early tonight."

"What a guy," Alice said.

"Be right up!" Kelly called back.

"And bring out the box of meat from the freezer that's marked for Mrs. Rawlings," Ron continued. "It's on the shelf about halfway back on the right."

"Okay."

Kelly and Alice got up. They crossed the lounge and headed up the steps. At the top, Alice headed toward the back door and Kelly turned to her left and pulled open the heavy door to the walk-in freezer.

The temperature inside was kept at a frigid minus twenty degrees Fahrenheit to keep the meats, ice creams, and other goods frozen solid.

She shivered and hurried along the wall to the right. She found the box with *Rawlings* scrawled in large, black letters and pulled it off the shelf.

That's when she heard the heavy freezer door slam behind her.

"Hey, leave it open, okay?" she called out.

The door remained closed.

"Hey, I'm in here!"

Kelly carried the box to the door and pushed on the plunger-type opener that unlatched the door.

Nothing happened. She was stuck inside the freezer.

Only then did she realize what had happened. Somebody arranged for this to happen. Someone wanted her locked inside.

And she didn't have to wonder who that was.

Chapter 11

"Hey! Somebody let me out of here!"

Kelly pushed on the opener again. The door didn't move.

That didn't make sense. The freezer didn't have a lock on it, and it had openers on the inside as well as the outside of the door.

Kelly put the box of meat on the floor and threw all of her weight against the door again. She could see the latch moving, but the door didn't budge.

Jeremy must have shoved something heavy in front of the door.

She shivered in the cold.

"Hey! Jeremy, let me out of here!"

She banged on the door.

"Hey! I'm going to freeze to death!"

Of course, that may very well be what he had in mind. Kelly was hoping someone else would hear and open the door.

The cold was getting almost unbearable now. The temperature outside was an Indian summer sixty degrees, so she was wearing only a cotton skirt and blouse under her work smock. She jumped up and down and rubbed her arms, trying to keep warm.

"Jeremy, everybody will know you locked me in

here!" she yelled. She banged again on the door with her fist.

The freezer door was so thick and the fans circulating the frigid air so noisy, that she couldn't hear anything outside the freezer. She wondered how much of her screaming could be heard on the other side.

"*Jeremy!*" she screamed, pounding the door. "*Jeremy!*

Kelly glanced at her watch. Two minutes had gone by since Ron called her upstairs. Surely, he would notice soon that she hadn't returned. Mrs. Rawlings must be standing just outside his office waiting for the box of meat. Ron was a good businessman, and he stressed to his employees that service was an important part of the job. In a few minutes he would, himself, come to find out why the meat had not been delivered to the front of the store.

"Hey! Somebody let me out of here!"

Then, through the thick walls of the freezer, she heard a very faint noise, a soft scraping sound.

The door of the freezer was flung open.

And there stood Jeremy Watts. He frowned, but there was a little smile at the corners of his mouth as if he couldn't quite mask his true feelings.

"What are you doing in there?"

Ron walked up behind him as she rushed out of the frigid air.

"Kelly, what's keeping you? Mrs. Rawlings has been waiting for nearly five minutes!"

"Somebody locked me in the freezer," Kelly said, staring straight at Jeremy.

"What are you talking about?" Ron said. "There's no lock on the freezer."

"I couldn't get out," Kelly said, still trembling with the cold. "I yelled and yelled and banged on the door."

"I heard the banging," Jeremy said, "when I came back here to use the bathroom."

"Somebody put something very heavy in front of the door," Kelly said. "I couldn't push it open."

Ron looked around him. There were shelves of grocery items surrounding them, but there was nothing large and heavy enough to block the freezer door.

"Maybe the latch stuck," he said. "I'll have someone come and look—"

"The latch didn't stick!" Kelly interrupted emphatically. "Somebody wanted me locked inside."

Ron shook his head as if this was too much to believe. He stepped inside the freezer and picked up the box from the floor.

"Jeremy, take the meat out to Mrs. Rawlings," he said. "She's already paid for it."

"It was a good thing I came along when I did," Jeremy said. "Kelly, you could've frozen to death." He continued to smile at Kelly, which infuriated her.

Jeremy took the box and disappeared through the swinging metal doors into the store.

"Ron, someone wanted me locked in the freezer," Kelly repeated.

"I just don't understand why you couldn't get out."

"Someone pushed something heavy—"

"There isn't anything that heavy around here."

"Well, I couldn't get the door open."

"Who do you think would do a thing like that to you?" Ron asked.

Kelly hesitated. How could she tell Ron it was Jeremy? Did she have any proof at all to back up any of her hunches about him? About the robberies? About the murders? About the tires slashed on her car? And now the freezer?

No, she had absolutely nothing to offer as evidence. In fact, it was Jeremy who had "rescued" her from the freezer. It was he who had said he heard her banging on the door, calling for help. If she accused Jeremy of locking her in the freezer, Ron would just point out that Jeremy first heard her cries for help.

"I don't know for sure," Kelly said. "But I *was* locked inside, Ron. Someone slammed the door behind me and kept me in there."

"Okay." Ron awkwardly patted her on the shoulder. He obviously didn't believe her, but he didn't want to say so. "Are you all right now? Have you warmed up?"

"Yes. I'll get back to work."

"Okay." He looked relieved.

Kelly sighed heavily and went back to work.

Kelly didn't see Miles until the end of school the next day. She had looked for him in the cafeteria at lunch and in the halls without luck, but she finally saw him strolling down the corridor near her locker after school.

She hurried after him.

"Miles!" she called. "Wait up a second."

Miles stopped and turned toward her.

Kelly caught up with him. "Miles, I owe you a huge apology. I'm so sorry I thought you'd stolen the motorcycle helmet. I don't know why I jumped to conclusions like that, but I hope you'll forgive me."

Miles didn't respond. He gazed off at something in the distance, away from Kelly.

"Miles? I'm really sorry."

When Miles still didn't say anything, Kelly assumed he was so angry he wasn't speaking to her.

"Okay," she said, "I guess I deserve the silent treatment. Anyway, I'm sorry."

She turned and started off down the hall.

"Kelly?"

Kelly turned back.

"Come with me."

Miles walked down the stairs next to the main office. Kelly followed him down another hall toward the music and P.E. areas.

By now, the corridors were practically deserted. The walls of the hall leading to the vocal rooms were lined with colorful posters for the upcoming production of *The Music Man,* but there were no students in sight. The only people remaining in the building were teachers, custodians, and those students involved in after-school activities, and they were already in the gym and rehearsal areas. There were no stragglers hanging around the halls at this end of the building.

When Miles turned down a short corridor that held nothing more than custodian's rooms, Kelly asked, "Where are we going?"

Miles turned to her and put a finger over his lips, signaling her to be quiet. He stopped at the end of the corridor before a small door that was only waist high.

Miles took out a key from his pocket and inserted it into the lock on the doorknob. He turned the key, withdrew it, then slowly, carefully opened the door.

"Alice in Wonderland?" Kelly whispered, nodding to the small door.

Miles smiled a little, shook his head, and backed through the doorway. The small door didn't open onto a room, but to a tunnel below with a ladder leading downward.

Miles started down the ladder and beckoned her to follow. She hadn't heard about this doorway or the tunnel under the school. She backed up to the ladder, too, and started down.

"Close the door behind you," Miles whispered.

She swung the door closed and descended the short ladder to the bottom.

"What *is* this?" she asked softly, looking around her.

They were surrounded by a brightly lit concrete corridor. It was quiet as a tomb down here, under the school, and it felt stuffy and close.

"There're a series of tunnels under the school," Miles said. "They lead to the other end of the building, out into the playing field, and into the parking lot."

"Why are they here?"

Miles shrugged and pointed to large pipes running along the top of the tunnel. "I suppose for maintenance crews."

"How did you find this place?"

Miles grinned. "When I was in ninth grade, I heard the principal was looking for me. I saw the door and it was unlocked. So I *disappeared.*"

"Is this where you go during school? Is that why I never see you during the day?"

"Sometimes I go to class."

"But most of the time you're down here?"

Miles didn't answer. "I want to show you something."

He took her hand and led her deeper into the tunnel. There were bulbs screwed into light sockets along the walls at regular intervals, so as they walked, they passed through spaces that were bright, then dim, then bright again.

"Where are we going?"

"You'll see."

Kelly had a fleeting thought that if Miles were really crazy, as Colette had thought, she could be in danger. The tunnel was unknown by other students, as far as Kelly knew, and it certainly appeared to be deserted now. She was completely alone with Miles. No one knew they were here. No one would ever try to look for her underground.

But Kelly felt safe with Miles. She had seen displays of his bad temper twice, but she didn't think he was dangerous.

They walked for another minute, and the tunnel abruptly stopped. There, in the corner, on an old rag rug was a pile of paperbacks, a denim jacket, several cans of soda, and a large vinyl case.

Miles grinned and gestured to the corner. "Have a seat."

"What is this?" Kelly sat down on the rug.

"Home away from home." Miles stretched out next to her on his stomach.

"No one has found this place of yours?"

"Not yet. I usually take everything with me when I leave." He leaned on his elbow and rested his head in his hand. "As long as the building doesn't have a major problem with its ventilation or plumbing systems, there's no reason for even the custodians to come down here."

"I can't believe this! You spend time down here every day?"

"Sometimes I sleep here." His smile faded. "It isn't always so great at home."

Kelly remembered the drunken man who had answered the telephone last night.

"I'm sorry."

Miles shrugged but didn't say anything.

"Where did you get the key to the tunnel?"

"Borrowed it and made a copy."

"Is that how you got into my locker? With a master key that you 'borrowed' from the custodians?"

"Uh-huh."

"Miles, if you put all that ingenuity—"

"—into something productive . . ." he said with her.

Kelly laughed. "Heard that before, huh?"

"Yeah."

Kelly pointed to the ladder and door above them. "Where does that lead?"

"It opens up in a big storage room next to the media center."

"We could've come down that way."

"Maybe. But sometimes the custodians have coffee in there this time of day."

Kelly's gaze fell on the black vinyl case. "What's in there? It looks like a musical instrument or something."

Miles looked over his shoulder. "It's a sax."

"You play the saxophone?"

"Not very well. I found it at Goodwill."

"Play it for me."

"Why?"

"I just want to hear you play."

"No. I've never had even one lesson."

"So what?"

"No."

There was a long silence.

"Daryl and I used to come down here in these tunnels," Miles said. "We were the only students who knew about them." He looked up at her. "Until you."

"You miss Daryl a lot, don't you?"

"Yeah." Miles closed his eyes and rolled over on his back, his hands behind his head. "I'd give anything to find out what happened the night he was killed. Anything."

Kelly thought about Jeremy and her suspicions. She wanted to share her thoughts about him with Miles, but she was afraid that Miles would do something awful to Jeremy. Maybe he deserved it, but she didn't know for *sure* that Jeremy was guilty. What if she was as wrong about him as she was about Miles stealing the motorcycle helmet?

Besides, Kelly didn't believe in revenge.

"Miles," she said carefully, "if we found out what happened—or who killed Daryl—we should go to the police and let them investigate and charge him with murder."

Miles looked up at her. "Did you find out something?"

"No, but after what you said the other day—"

Miles sat up. "You know something, don't you?"

"No, I don't know anything." She'd never been a good liar, but she tried her hardest not to give herself away.

"You suspect someone though. From the market?"

"No. Really, Miles. I don't know anything."

Miles sat back, disappointment evident on his face.

"You and Daryl were really close, weren't you?" Kelly said softly.

"Yeah. He and I—we knew each other real well. We didn't even have to talk in complete sentences. He'd say a few words, and I knew what he was going to say. Sometimes we'd finish each other's sentences."

"He must've been a lot like you," Kelly said.

"Yeah, he was."

Kelly smiled. "Then I would have liked him."

Miles gazed over at her a moment. Then he reached over and gently touched her cheek.

"I've never met a girl like you," he said.

She couldn't stifle her giggle. "Well, I certainly have never met a guy like *you!*"

His arms encircled her, and he pulled her to him. They sat there together for a few minutes, enjoying the closeness of each other.

"Did you play the sax for Daryl?"

"Yeah."

"Then play for me. Please?"

Miles released her and grinned. "I can't say no to you, Kelly. But first, I have to check and see if anybody's up in the storage room. They could hear the sax."

He climbed nimbly up the ladder, opened the door a crack, and peeked out.

"It's okay. Nobody's there," he said after he closed the door and leaped from the ladder.

He opened the case, pulled out the sax, fixed the mouthpiece and reed in place, and played.

Kelly was astounded. Miles was a natural musician. He played with sensitivity and passion, his eyes closed, losing himself in the mournful blues melody. His sax became a part of him, expressing the melancholy and sadness of his life more eloquently than words ever could.

When he finished, the music fading into silence, Kelly couldn't speak for a moment. She had been moved, not just by the music, but by knowing that Miles had bought the old sax secondhand, had taught himself to play, and had brought the instrument here to his special, private place. And that he had shared it all with her.

"That was beautiful, Miles," she said finally. "Really beautiful. How long have you been playing?"

There was a light in Miles's eyes, and Kelly knew he was very pleased with her response to his music.

"About seven years."

A noise from over their heads startled them. The door was opening. Miles jumped up and gave Kelly a shove.

"Run to the other end!" he whispered urgently. "I'm right behind you."

Kelly was aware that Miles turned back to grab his sax case, so she scooped up the rug and headed off through the tunnel. The two of them ran as fast as they could, and they didn't stop running until they reached safety at the other end.

Chapter 12

"Hi, Mrs. Talbot. How are you this evening?"

Jeremy grinned at the woman wearing blue slacks and a fancy sweatshirt that said "Sixty Something" spelled out in glittering rhinestones.

Jeremy was working at cash register four next to Kelly. Colette was at register two and Alice was working at register three. Jeremy's back was toward Kelly, so she could watch him without him being aware of it.

"Just fine, Jeremy," Mrs. Talbot said pleasantly. "You're busier than usual tonight."

"Yes, ma'am, we are," he said.

He turned to the boy who was sacking for Kelly. "Jeff, I need a sacker here."

Kelly didn't have a customer at the moment, so Jeff nodded and moved down to help Jeremy.

"How is your husband doing today?" Jeremy asked Mrs. Talbot.

"Oh, he's better," Mrs. Talbot said wearily. "But the doctor says he has to stay at the hospital for at least several more days. Maybe longer. Bypass surgery takes a lot out of a person."

"Well, I hope he's back on his feet again real soon."

Jeremy took Mrs. Talbot's check and tendered out the order. "Thanks, Mrs. Talbot." He handed her the receipt.

"Thank you, Jeremy."

She and Jeff walked out of the store together, Jeff wheeling the grocery cart in front of him.

An elderly man approached Kelly's register and placed a box of hot cereal and a carton of milk on the counter. Kelly smiled at him and rang up the items.

"That'll be $3.72, please."

While she waited for the man to pull the money out of his wallet, Kelly glanced over at Jeremy. He was leaning over his counter writing on a pad of paper.

Then he straightened up and tossed a check into the cash register.

Kelly's heart slammed hard against her ribs. Jeremy had just copied something from Mrs. Talbot's check.

Did he copy her address? *Was she his next burglary victim?*

Did Jeremy think that while poor Mr. Talbot was recuperating in the hospital from his heart bypass operation, he could break into the Talbot's house and rob them?

Jeremy ripped off the small piece of paper from the pad, folded it, and shoved it into the pocket of his Corner Market smock.

The old man at Kelly's register handed her his check and she finished the sale and handed him the receipt. He thanked her and left.

She glanced over at Jeremy again. He was scanning items for another customer.

If only she could get hold of that paper on which Jeremy had copied the check's information. It could be the proof she needed to go to the police.

Kelly wished she were a pickpocket so she could gently lift the paper out of Jeremy's smock pocket without his knowing it.

She knew there was no way she could pull that off.

Maybe Jeremy would take off the smock during his break and she could get the paper then. He was supposed to take a break very soon.

Kelly rang up three more customers before Ron called out to Jeremy that he should take his fifteen minutes now.

Kelly was scanning a large order for a mother with three dirty-faced kids waiting behind her, but she glanced over at Jeremy every couple of seconds, hoping he would take off his smock.

Finally Jeremy did just that, whipping it off and tossing it on the counter behind him. Then he headed down the aisle toward the back of the store.

What luck. He hadn't taken the slip of paper from the pocket before he left. At least, she didn't think he had. If she could just get hold of it . . .

"Leave that alone!" the mother snapped at her youngest child, who had picked up a candy bar from the wire stand next to the cash register. The little boy paid no attention and tore open the paper wrapper.

"I said NO!" yelled the mother. She smacked him hard on his butt, and the store was immediately filled with the sound of his loud wails. She looked at Kelly and shook her head. "Kids," she mumbled disgustedly.

Kelly finished ringing up the woman's order as quickly as she could, keeping one eye on the smock that Jeremy had tossed aside so carelessly.

The mother finally walked out with her noisy brood.

Now was Kelly's chance.

She glanced over her shoulder to make sure

Jeremy wasn't in sight, then quickly moved around her counter and over to where Jeremy had been working.

She stood over the smock on the counter, her heart *tha-rumping* hard in her chest, and reached for the pocket.

"Kelly, come sack for me." Alice's voice startled her. "My sacker's on break, and I can't keep up with this."

"Okay," Kelly said. She glanced down at the apron and didn't move. She'd wait until Alice turned away again, and then she'd grab the paper.

Alice scowled. "Come *on,* what're you waiting for?" Cranky Alice wasn't going to turn away. She was used to getting what she wanted *when* she wanted it.

Kelly sighed and hurried over to sack for her. It didn't look as if she would get the paper now.

Maybe she'd still have a chance to get it before Jeremy returned from his break.

But it didn't work out that way. The store stayed busy, and Kelly continued to sack for Alice. Ron came out of his office to work at Kelly's register, and before long Jeremy returned from his break, pulling the smock on and buttoning it down the front.

So much for getting evidence for the police. She'd never get it now.

After an hour of sacking, Kelly returned to her register. Jeremy was busy scanning at his counter. Her gaze fell on the pad of paper he'd used when he wrote down Mrs. Talbot's check information, and a thought occurred to her.

What if Jeremy pressed hard enough that his writing left an impression on the page directly underneath, the page that was now on the top of the pad?

Wouldn't that evidence be just as convincing for the police?

But how was she going to get the pad of paper?

Could she simply ask Jeremy if he had some paper she could use? She could tell him she was going to order some—what would it be?—maybe some frozen yogurt for a customer. He wouldn't suspect why she really wanted it. Would he?

It was worth a try.

She glanced down and spotted her own pad on the counter next to her. She grabbed it and tossed it into the wastebasket next to her.

"Jeremy?" she called.

He turned to look at her.

"Could I use your notepad? I just remembered that Mrs. Jenkins wanted some yogurt, and I forgot to write it down."

Jeremy picked up his notepad and tossed it to her.

That couldn't have been easier!

Kelly smiled to herself, thinking he'd just thrown her some evidence that just might throw *him* in prison.

She tore off the top page and pocketed it in her smock, then pretended to write out the order for Mrs. Jenkins.

Ron poked his head out of the booth.

"Colette, you've had your break, right?"

"Right."

"Alice, you too?"

"Yup."

"Jeremy's had his. Kelly, it's your turn."

"Okay." Kelly was glad for the rest, and she was anxious to get the torn page from Jeremy's pad into a safe place.

She hurried to the booth and slipped the page into

her purse. She'd have to wait until she got home tonight to look at it carefully under the light. Maybe she'd scribble lightly with pencil over the impression of Jeremy's letters so they could be seen more easily by the police.

She then walked to the back of the store and headed lightheartedly down the stairs. She was turning into quite a good detective, and she felt very proud that she was doing something that could stop the robberies and murder.

She wouldn't have to get Miles involved. She could give him the good news after she'd delivered her evidence to the police. Miles wouldn't feel he needed to get even with Jeremy for Daryl's death if the police charged Jeremy with the robberies and began questioning him for the murders of Daryl and Craig.

It made her feel good to have performed so well in her self-appointed detective job.

But she didn't have long to feel good.

Halfway down the stairs the step under her gave way. She screamed and grabbed for the railing, but missed it, and tumbled headfirst into the basement.

Chapter 13

The world turned and spun around her and didn't stop somersaulting until she found herself lying on the floor staring at the ceiling.

She lay there a few moments, dazed. She struggled to bring her mind into focus.

What had happened? What was she doing on the floor? Wasn't this the employee lounge at the Corner Market? She tried to make sense of it.

Her head was throbbing with a monster of a headache. She must have bumped it on the way down. She had a crazy vision of someone bouncing her head like a basketball down the basement steps.

Bounce . . . bounce . . . bounce. With every bounce, her head pulsated with pain.

She slid her arm over an inch, and it ached terribly. She stopped attempting to move and lay there, trying to decide what to do next.

Kelly knew that no one would hear her if she yelled, unless one of the other employees happened to be standing at the top of the stairs. That was unlikely, unless someone had run back to use the rest room. Even then, they wouldn't stop at the top of the stairs. They be hurrying by and thinking about something else. They'd never hear her yell.

She didn't feel like yelling, anyway.

She moved her other arm experimentally and found that it didn't hurt. Her legs were very sore, but other than that they were okay, too. She struggled to sit up, leaning on her good arm for balance.

A wave of nausea washed over her, but she was so determined to get up off the cement floor that she gritted her teeth until the feeling had passed.

After several minutes and with great difficulty, she managed to get to her feet. She hobbled over to the stairway and pulled herself up five of the steps.

She stopped in front of the step that had given way under her weight. It had broken at the edge as if years of tromping feet had weakened the wood.

How could that have happened? It was true, these stairs were old and a little rickety, but how could the edge of the stair just fall away like that?

She leaned down to examine the wood, and her heart leaped into her throat.

This was no accident. *The wood had been cut— there was a fresh saw mark—vertically in the step so that very little weight on it would tear the step away from the rest of the structure.*

She sat there on the step and turned her thoughts to Jeremy. He had to be responsible for this. Who else would have wanted her to fall and possibly crack her head open? Jeremy had taken his break earlier, but so had everyone else. Had he left any other time during the evening? She tried to remember.

Yes, he had. He'd left to use the rest room not very long ago.

He'd been gone long enough to saw through the wood on the step.

First the freezer, and now the step.

He's playing with me, Kelly thought. He's already murdered two people, Daryl and Craig, one by running him down with a car, the other by slitting his throat.

But *why* is he just playing with me? He must know I know about him. Why is he trying to scare me or injure me when he could just kill me outright like the others?

It didn't make sense.

"Kelly?" Colette's head appeared at the top of the stairs. "Why are you sitting there?"

"I fell," Kelly said, glad to see her friend. "The step . . . gave way."

Should she tell Colette about the step? About the freezer? Was it time to confide her suspicions about Jeremy?

Yes, she thought it was. But not right now. Not here, when anybody could appear unexpectedly, when Colette would have a million questions.

"Oh, my gosh! Are you okay?" Colette hurried down the steps. She reached out. "Here, let me help you. Give me your arm."

Colette put Kelly's arm around her neck and she helped her climb the stairs. At the top, she dragged a metal chair over from under the wall phone and eased Kelly into it.

"I'll get Ron," she said. "You should go home."

Alice brought Kelly's car to the curb next to the store, and Colette helped Kelly ease into the driver's seat. Ron stood on the sidewalk frowning with concern.

"You sure you can drive, kiddo?" he asked, leaning into the passenger's side window.

"I'm fine," Kelly said. "Really."

When Colette had brought Ron back from his booth after the accident, Kelly had whispered to him, "Look at the step, Ron. *Look* at it, okay?"

He had nodded grimly and then helped her to her feet.

Kelly hoped that when he saw the fresh cut in the old wood, he'd realize that her getting locked in the freezer was no accident, either.

And, in spite of her awful fall down the stairs, she now had proof about the burglaries, she thought triumphantly. Colette had brought Kelly her purse, which contained the page from Jeremy's pad, and it lay on the passenger seat next to her.

Kelly pulled away from the curb next to the store. She waved good-bye to Colette, Ron, and Alice, and drove the seven miles home.

She pulled her old station wagon into the barn and climbed painfully out of the car. Taking a deep breath, she straightened up and forced herself to take long, deliberate steps toward the house. She wanted to look as normal as possible when her grandparents saw her so they wouldn't worry. She loved them so much, and she didn't want to put extra strain on Grandad's heart.

"Kelly, what a surprise!" her grandmother said, turning from the kitchen sink when she walked in. "Aren't you home awfully early?"

"Yes," Kelly said. "I stumbled going down the stairs at work, so Ron said I could come home—"

"Oh, my dear, are you all right?" Nana hurried over and gazed worriedly into her granddaughter's face.

"Sure." Kelly shrugged. "It was no big deal. I'll have a scratch or two and a couple of bruises, but other than that I'm fine."

"Oh, I hope so, honey. Do you need some help getting upstairs?"

"No. Really, I'm fine."

"Well, okay, if you say so. Oh, I almost forgot

again!" Nana said, thumping herself on the side of the head. "There was an envelope for you in the mail this morning. The postmark was from Spencer Point, so I knew it wasn't from any of your old friends, and I just forgot to give it to you. I'm so sorry, dear."

"That's okay. Where is it?"

"I put it on the desk in your room."

"Thanks, Nana. I think I'll go up and take a bath and then get to bed. I'm really tired."

"Fine, dear. We're heading up to bed soon, ourselves. Good night. I hope you're not so sore in the morning."

"I hope so, too. 'Night."

Kelly climbed the stairs slowly and walked into her room, switching on the light.

If I sit down now, I'll never get up again, she thought, dropping her purse on the bed.

She leaned over and unzipped the leather bag. She was anxious to look at that page under the bright light on her desk. Then, if she could see Jeremy's words impressed on the paper, she'd take it to the police tomorrow. That, along with the sawed stair, ought to be enough for the police to start questioning Jeremy.

Kelly fumbled around in her purse.

"I left it right on top," she murmured.

It wasn't there.

Maybe it had slipped down one side or the other when she pulled out her car keys, she thought. She slid her hand along the leather interior. She felt her wallet, a hairbrush, a tissue, her keys, and a roll of Life Savers.

But no small piece of paper.

She turned her purse over and dumped the contents out on her bed, then sat down and rummaged through the items.

"I put it here!" she said aloud. "Just before my break. I'm *positive!*"

But the paper was gone.

Someone—Jeremy, for sure—had stolen it right out of her purse, perhaps while she lay in pain on the basement floor.

Could he have gone through her purse in Ron's booth without anyone seeing? It would have been difficult. Ron was in the booth when Kelly left to go down for her break.

Colette had brought her the purse just before she'd left the store. Could *she* have taken—

Oh, that was a stupid thought! What reason would Colette have for stealing the paper from her? She wouldn't have wanted to protect Jeremy. She didn't even like him. For that matter, neither did anyone else.

So Jeremy had to have been the thief. Somehow, he got into the booth when no one was looking and took it from her purse. He must have figured out why she wanted the pad while she was taking her break. So sometime while she was downstairs he stole the paper from her purse.

What was she going to do now? She'd lost her proof that Jeremy was responsible for the break-ins. The only evidence she had left was the freshly cut stair, but she had no evidence linking Jeremy to that.

Kelly was devastated. Some detective she was turning out to be. She'd allowed her best piece of evidence to be stolen from her. How was she going to convince the police now that Jeremy was a thief and a murderer?

She gazed across her room, and noticed the white envelope propped up against her desk lamp. She eased herself off the bed, then walked over and picked it up.

KELLY MCLEES, it said in small capital letters. The address was written in the same kindergarten hand.

What's this? An imaginative invitation or something, she guessed.

She tore open the envelope and a piece of paper fluttered to the floor. It was newsprint.

Kelly leaned over, groaning with pain, and picked it up.

It took a second for Kelly to realize what was in her hand. When it registered, her heart slammed into her ribs and her palms slicked with sweat.

Kelly held in her hand the picture of herself from the school paper. The two boys on either side had been cut away and only her form remained.

A string was tied around the neck of her picture in a hangman's noose. It was drawn so tightly that her head and neck were curled into a tight roll.

Her picture was taped to another piece of paper. On that paper, in the same capital letters, it said MIND YOUR OWN BUSINESS UNLESS YOU WANT TO DIE.

Chapter 14

Kelly found Miles sitting on the hood of her car after school the next day. They'd spotted each other across the lot, and he watched her intently as she threaded her way through the crowded student parking area.

Kelly smiled warmly as she approached him. "Hi, Miles."

In spite of all that had happened to her since Miles had taken her into the underground tunnel, Kelly had been thinking about him a lot. She played over in her mind the way they had sat together on the rug, the way he had played the saxophone, the way he had touched her cheek.

She remembered Colette's warning not to play social worker with Miles. Kelly wondered if her growing feelings for Miles might stem from her need to help people, to make things all right. Was Miles just a "project" to her, a challenge, a wild animal to tame?

She didn't want to think that Colette might be right. True, when she heard the voice of his drunken father, she felt immediate sympathy for Miles, and she'd decided then and there that she shouldn't judge him.

But when she heard Miles play the saxophone, she

was overwhelmed with awe and respect for his talent. And when he touched her cheek, she certainly wasn't thinking of him as a *charity case*.

Miles didn't return her smile. "Hi, yourself."

"You okay?"

Miles jumped down from the hood, and taking her chin in his hand, turned her head to one side.

"Where did you get that bruise on your face?"

Kelly's hand instinctively went to her cheek.

"I—I fell."

"Where?"

"At work. On the stairs."

"How'd it happen?"

"The step broke, I guess. The stairs are pretty old."

"That's not what I heard." Miles released her and stepped back, folding his arms over his chest. He leaned back, resting against the hood of the car.

Kelly was aware that the crowd in the parking lot was thinning out. She glanced around to make sure there was no one listening nearby.

"What do you mean?"

"The stair was cut, wasn't it, Kelly?"

Kelly stared at him, astounded. "How did you know?"

"I overheard your good friends talking, Colette and Alice. They were in line for lunch before you arrived. They didn't know I was behind them. Colette said she overheard you tell the store manager that he should check the step. So she looked at it after work. She said it had been cut clean through with a saw."

Kelly didn't know what to say. She'd seen both Colette and Alice today, and neither had mentioned the stairs or the accident. *Why not?*

"What's going on, Kelly?"

She could see the anger brewing in Miles's face.

"I don't know for sure what's going on," Kelly said slowly. "But I have a hunch."

"Who cut the stair?"

"I'm not sure—but I think one of the guys who works there."

"What's his name?"

"His name's Jeremy Watts," Kelly said. "But Miles, I don't have any proof that would stand up in court. I don't even have enough information that would interest the police. Besides, maybe someone else was supposed to fall. Or maybe it was just a practical joke."

"Uh-huh." Miles clearly didn't believe that.

"I can't be *sure* about any of this," Kelly said.

"Why would he want to hurt you?" Miles pressed.

"Maybe he thinks I know something," Kelly said, "about the murders."

"Do you?"

Kelly shook her head. "All I have are guesses."

"You think Jeremy killed Daryl and Craig?" Miles said.

"I don't know," Kelly said. "I just don't know. I have absolutely nothing to go on."

"I think you're in danger," Miles said.

"No," Kelly said. "If he'd wanted me dead, he would have killed me. I think he's trying to scare me because I've been asking questions."

"Then stop asking questions," Miles said. "Let me do some checking on this Jeremy Watts."

"What are you going to do?"

"Find out what I can about him."

"*You* be careful," Kelly said. "Okay?"

"Sure," Miles said.

He walked Kelly around the car to the driver's side. She got in.

"You work tonight?" he asked.

"Yes."

"Watch yourself."

"I will," she said.

"Better than last night. I wish I could be there to protect you."

She smiled. "Don't worry." He nodded to her and she drove out of the lot toward home.

"Remember when you told me Jeremy was a jerk?" Kelly said.

Colette nodded. She took a sip of her Coke. "He is."

The girls were taking their break in the basement employee lounge. Kelly had decided to start a conversation with Colette about Jeremy to see where it would lead, but she wanted to be careful. She still wasn't sure Colette could be trusted. Colette was awfully friendly with Alice, and Kelly was *sure* Alice wasn't trustworthy.

"Yeah, I think so, too," Kelly said, fingering the empty paper cup in front of her. "What do you think his problem is?"

Colette shrugged. "Who knows? Maybe his parents are ax murderers." She grinned, not knowing how close her joke had come to a possible truth about Jeremy.

"What do you think Jeremy is capable of doing?" Kelly said.

"You mean, like sawing through a step to cause an accident?" Colette took another sip from her cup.

- Kelly watched her carefully. "That's right."

"Do you think Jeremy did that?" Colette asked.

"I don't know who else might have done it. Do you?"

"No. But why Jeremy? And why would he want to hurt *you?*"

"Maybe he doesn't like me."

"Jeremy doesn't like anybody."

"Except the women who come in here."

"I still think he's trying to get written into somebody's will," Colette said with a smile. "He doesn't actually *like* those women."

"Maybe there's another reason he's being nice."

"What's that?"

Kelly paused, running her finger over the lip of the cup. Then she decided to take the plunge, to tell Colette what she knew. But she wanted to choose her words carefully.

"Remember the last burglary around here? Mr. and Mrs. Hawkins?"

"Right. She shops here at the store."

"I know. Several days before the robbery, I overheard Mrs. Hawkins talking to Jeremy about her trip to Europe."

"Boy, he really butters up those women!" Colette said, rolling her eyes. "He makes them think he's really interested in their lives. What a hypocrite."

"Jeremy asked her when she was leaving, and she told him."

"Yeah?"

"Their conversation was out in the parking lot where no one would hear them. Except I overheard it."

"Uh-huh?" Colette was waiting for more.

"Then she left on vacation, and their home was robbed."

"Yeah."

Kelly stopped and stared at Colette. "Don't you think there could be a connection?"

"Between what and what? You mean, Jeremy talking to Mrs. Hawkins and the robbery?"

Kelly suddenly felt very foolish. "Well, there could be—"

"You think that *Jeremy* robbed the Hawkins couple?"

"It's possible."

"Well, yeah, I s'ppose, but it's a pretty big jump, Jeremy talking to Mrs. Hawkins about her vacation, and Jeremy breaking into her house and robbing her, don't you think? I mean, sure, he's an arrogant jerk, but I don't know about breaking and entering. That's a felony." She grinned. "I'm not sure he's smart enough to pull off a robbery, anyway. The police say those break-ins have been real well planned."

"But when Jeremy saw that I was listening to the conversation between him and Mrs. Hawkins, he told me to mind my own business."

"Jeremy says stuff like that all the time, Kelly. One day he accused me of having a big head because he heard me tell Alice that I'd gotten straight A's."

"But the stair—"

"Yeah, I don't know who did that," Colette said. "It sure *could've* been Jeremy. He's really a creep, all right, but I don't think your robbery theory holds up. I mean, I suppose it's possible, but then *anything's* possible."

Kelly felt deflated. Colette was right. Her accusations were without any validity. If her robbery theory didn't hold up, her suspicions about Craig's and Daryl's murders were even wilder.

She wished she'd kept her mouth shut. She was glad she hadn't accused Jeremy of locking her in the freezer or sending her threatening notes or slashing her tires. Colette was right about Jeremy being a creep, and she might even agree that Jeremy was *capable* of the harassment to which Kelly had been subjected lately.

But Colette was also right that Kelly had absolutely nothing to go on, nothing that could connect Jeremy with robbery—and certainly not murder.

"Kelly, will you meet me in my office?" Ron's voice boomed out over the intercom.

"Sure, be right up." Kelly turned back to Colette. "You're right," she said. "I don't have good evidence that Jeremy is burglarizing those homes, but I still think he's involved."

Colette shrugged and smiled. "Maybe. See you later."

Kelly walked to the bottom of the stairs. A movement out the corner of her eye caught her attention. She turned to her left and saw Jeremy standing next to the employees' coat locker.

He obviously had been standing there, listening to her conversation with Colette. His face was dark and fierce and angry.

"Hello, babe." His voice was menacing, but so soft that Colette couldn't have heard.

Kelly didn't respond.

Her heart thundering against her ribs, she hurried up the stairs.

Chapter 15

He heard everything! Kelly thought desperately, hurrying on trembling legs toward the front of the store. *He warned me in his note to mind my own business, and now he knows I'm talking to other people about him and the robberies!*

Why hadn't she been more careful?

What would Jeremy do to her? Would he kill her? He might have already killed two people who figured out the connection between him and the robberies.

Should she believe his note? Would she be the next to die because she hadn't minded her own business?

Kelly found Ron in his booth, sitting behind his desk. He looked up when she walked in.

"Come in, Kelly, and close the door behind you."

She swung the door closed and sat down in the chair on the opposite side of his desk.

"I looked at the stair that broke when you stepped on it," Ron said. "Since you asked me to examine it, I suppose you know that it was cut nearly all the way across with a saw."

"Yes."

Kelly's mind was whirling. She knew what question was coming: *Do you know who did it?*

What would she say? After her conversation with

Colette, she knew that if she accused Jeremy of being responsible, she wouldn't be able to convince Ron of his guilt. She had no proof.

If she did point the accusing finger at Jeremy, Ron's second question would certainly be *Why would Jeremy want to hurt you?*

Without evidence, she couldn't accuse Jeremy of breaking into the wealthy homes in this area, and she certainly couldn't suggest that Jeremy was a murderer! She'd look even more foolish than she had downstairs with Colette.

"I've thought some more about what you said about getting stuck in the freezer," Ron said.

"Yes."

A worry line creased Ron's forehead. He fiddled with a pencil on his desk.

"Do you have any reason to believe that both of these things were directed at you personally?"

"Any reason?"

Ron nodded.

"Well—" She stared at the floor.

If she told Ron she thought Jeremy *might* be responsible, he would certainly talk to Jeremy about it. He'd ask Jeremy if he liked Kelly, if they got along. Jeremy wouldn't need to wonder why Ron was asking. He'd know Kelly had talked to Ron about him, just as she had with Colette.

Jeremy would just be more careful not to be anywhere nearby when the next "accident" happened.

Maybe Jeremy would just *finish* the job once and for all.

"Kelly?" Ron was watching her intently, waiting for an answer.

"No, I don't think these things have been against me, personally," Kelly said, still staring at the floor.

"Well, let me tell you what I'm going to do," Ron

said. "I'm calling a special employee meeting after work tomorrow. Everyone is to be here. I'm going to talk about the two incidents and warn everybody that if I discover who was responsible, that person will be fired immediately and the police will be notified."

"Okay."

"I'll also ask everyone to keep an eye out for any other 'pranks,' dangerous or not, against Market employees."

"Thanks, Ron."

Kelly was relieved. Jeremy will realize that she hadn't accused him of cutting the stair or locking her in the freezer. Maybe he'd leave her alone.

Or was that just wishful thinking?

"I'll walk out with you," Colette said to Kelly.

The girls had gotten their jackets from the lockers downstairs and were picking up their purses in Ron's booth at the end of the evening.

"What do you think the meeting's about?" Colette whispered to Kelly as they walked toward the front entrance. "Ron's never called an employee meeting in the middle of the month like this. Something must be up."

"Maybe," Kelly said vaguely. What good would it do to talk about it again?

They walked through the automatic doors. The parking lot was dark, and the smoky, sweet smells of autumn were in the evening air.

"What did Ron want to talk to you about after your break?"

"Oh—" *What should she say?* "He just wondered how I was feeling. I mean, after my fall down the stairs."

Colette giggled. "Maybe he's afraid you're going to sue him."

"I'd never do that."

"I know. You don't do what *normal* people do. You're too nice."

Kelly turned to look at Colette. That sounded like something Alice had said the other day. What was it? Oh yes, she'd called Kelly a bleeding heart. *So understanding. Always saying the right things. Always doing the right things.*

Alice had said it sarcastically, but Kelly wasn't sure how Colette meant it. Her tone of voice didn't give any clues.

"Well, good night," Kelly said.

"See you at school tomorrow."

The girls parted and walked to their own cars. Kelly climbed into her old station wagon and headed for home.

Colette's friendship with Alice puzzled Kelly. Colette seemed to be a friendly, cheerful, optimistic person most of the time. So why would she like Alice, who was just the opposite?

Did her comment about Kelly just now indicate that she and Alice had been talking about her? Did Colette tell Alice that Kelly suspected Jeremy of the robberies in Spencer Point?

If she did, the story was likely to be all over school the next day.

Kelly pulled up to the last stoplight on the edge of town. At ten o'clock on a weekday evening there usually wasn't a lot of traffic on the street, and tonight was no different.

She glanced in her rearview mirror and saw one car approaching slowly. The light turned green, so Kelly pulled into the intersection and headed down the street. This road was designated as Highway 52. It was a two-lane road and ran past her grandparents' house in the country seven miles away.

In spite of the chill, Kelly lowered her window an inch to smell the sweet night air. She enjoyed the drive home every night. It was a time to relax, and it provided a buffer zone of sorts between the working day and bedtime at home.

Lately, she had needed that ten minutes to unwind. She felt very tense around Jeremy. Since he had locked her in the freezer, she had been on guard whenever he was around, and that was nearly all the time.

She was very glad that Ron was going to warn everybody about further "pranks," as he called them. She hoped Jeremy would realize she had no proof against him, and know that she hadn't pointed the accusing finger at him when she talked to Ron.

Maybe he would leave her alone. Maybe he would relax and make another mistake that would provide proof against him.

If only she had been able to hold on to the slip of paper with the imprint of his next victim's address! She could have taken it to the police, and they would be investigating by now.

Kelly ran a hand through her hair and breathed in the sweet country air. Recently harvested corn fields lay on both sides of her as she drove swiftly down the narrow highway.

Sudden glaring lights reflected in her rearview mirror blinded Kelly. The driver in the car behind her had turned on his bright headlights. Assuming he was signaling that he was about to pass, Kelly slowed a little and ducked her head to avoid the reflection.

But the car didn't pass. It came up close behind her station wagon and banged into her rear bumper.

Kelly gasped and grabbed the wheel tightly to keep control of the car. She peered into the rearview mirror. There was only one person in the car behind her, a dark figure hunched over the steering wheel.

Was it Jeremy? She couldn't make out who it was. She couldn't even be sure of the driver's gender. A coat was pulled up around the driver's head and didn't reveal the shape of his—or her—head.

In the night, she couldn't recognize the car with its headlights glaring either.

Kelly trembled all over as adrenaline shot through her body.

Just keep your head, she told herself. *Keep control of the car.*

The car bumped her again from behind, only harder this time, throwing her backward to hit the headrest.

Now the car pulled out into the left lane as if to pass.

She slowed a little. "Just pass me, okay? Just pass me," she whispered.

She knew he would do no such thing. She felt a trickle of sweat run down her left side.

The car came up even with her station wagon. She glanced over, wanting to see the driver, wanting to be *sure* it was Jeremy.

But the driver's face was in shadows. The car was a dark color, but she couldn't distinguish the make.

He jerked his car to the right suddenly, violently, and banged hard into Kelly's car. She lost control as the car lunged to the edge of the road.

Kelly righted her car, but seconds later, he came back at her and slammed against her again with even more force. This time, when her car swerved to the right, it slammed into a postbox on the side of the road. The box snapped off its wooden post, and Kelly cried out as it crashed into her windshield.

The glass panel shattered, raining small pellets of

safety glass down into her face, and the wind roared into the front seat.

Kelly managed to edge the car back onto the road. *"Stop it, oh God, just leave me alone!"*

The wind blasted into her face, making breathing difficult. She gasped and choked and turned her head to the side to catch a breath.

This couldn't be happening.

But she knew it was, and she also knew that this time someone wasn't just playing with her. This was not a warning.

This was someone who wanted her dead.

Jeremy. It had to be Jeremy.

She peered ahead, hoping to see more traffic coming toward her. Surely he would get out of the left-hand lane if a car were heading toward him. That would buy her a little time.

But time for what? What would she do? Would she pull in the drive at her isolated country home? Wouldn't he follow her? What a perfect place for him to finish off what he'd started on the highway!

Up ahead came a short line of traffic heading her way. The car at her side slowed a bit and pulled back behind her. Kelly sighed heavily, knowing the driver wasn't through yet, and this pause in his attacks would be brief.

And it was. The driver came up behind and rammed her station wagon from behind for the third time. Her head snapped back again.

For a moment, she lost control of her car. When her head bounced upright again, she looked down the road, and was appalled to see that she had crossed the center line.

Huge headlights were speeding toward her.

A semi. She had only seconds before it would hit her head-on.

She screamed and the sound of it blended with the loud shriek of the truck's horn.

She jerked the steering wheel to the right, but saw headlights over her shoulder. *The car behind her had pulled up even with her, blocking access to the right lane.*

There was only one other way to go. With the semi almost upon her, she yanked the steering wheel to the left.

Something at the side of the road appeared in front of her out of the darkness.

A hay wagon.

She stood on her brakes and muscled the steering wheel as far left as she could.

Tires screeching, her car whipped into a tailspin as the semi barrelled by on the highway, not six feet from her.

Her car came to an abrupt stop, with Kelly facing the direction from which she had come. Miraculously, she hadn't hit the hay wagon.

Miraculously, she was alive.

The deadly car that had chased her down the highway was gone. It had disappeared into the gloom of night.

Chapter 16

Kelly sat in the farm drive with the wind whipping her face. She was still breathing hard and her heart drummed frantically.

What should she do now? Go to the police? She *still* couldn't prove who was responsible for the awful things that had happened to her, not even this attempt to kill her on the highway.

It *had* to have been Jeremy. He was determined to kill her because she suspected the truth about him.

If she went to the police, would they protect her? Without proof that Jeremy was responsible, would they be able to arrest him so he wouldn't be able to kill her?

She knew the answers to those questions. The police would begin an investigation, and in the meantime, Jeremy would be free to go to school, work at the Corner Market, and do whatever he wanted to do.

And what he wanted to do was kill her.

Kelly slumped in the car as the realization became clear. The police would provide no protection for her. Not even after what had happened tonight.

Protection. Kelly raised her head, a memory flooding her mind.

Miles. He had said he wanted to protect her.

Maybe she should go to him and tell him every-thing: about her suspicions that Jeremy was involved in the break-ins and the murders, about the slashed tires, the threatening note, and now the car that ran her off the road. They could go to the police together. Then, while the authorities were investigating, Miles would help her stay safely away from Jeremy.

That was it. She had to call Miles, to get hold of him. She needed a phone.

She checked the highway for traffic, then pulled back onto the road, heading back to town. She'd call her grandparents with yet another lie to explain her late homecoming. They would be horrified if they knew the truth, and there was no telling what the shock and worry would do to Grandad's heart. She had no choice. She *had* to lie.

The driving was difficult without a windshield. The cold wind slammed into her, taking her breath away, and blowing her hair wildly around her face.

Kelly stopped at a gas station on the edge of town, dialed her home phone from an outside booth, and explained to Nana that she was going to Colette's house to do some last-minute cramming for a math test tomorrow.

Then she looked up Miles's number and dialed. She let the phone ring twenty times before she hung up.

He wasn't home. Where was he?

Then she remembered. *The tunnel.* Miles was probably in the tunnel under the school. He'd told her he sleeps there when things get bad at home.

She checked her watch. It was 10:28. Would she be able to get into the school? The only way to find out was to drive out there.

Before getting back into the car, she quickly walked around it to see the damage. Besides losing the windshield, the car had two large dents in the back fender and the passenger's side door was pushed in. But she'd worry about fixing the damage later.

She got back into her car and headed toward school. She had to drive to the other side of town to reach the high school, and it took her nearly twenty minutes before she arrived.

There were lights on inside. Good. The custodians were still working.

She parked close to the building in the teachers' parking lot. She didn't bother to lock the door. The missing windshield left the car as vulnerable as if she had left her keys hanging in the outside lock, anyway.

Now she needed to find an open door to the school.

Kelly hurried to the closest entrance, which led into the corridor below the media center. It was locked.

Then she walked around to the front of the school and tried the door. It was locked too. So was the gym door.

A motorcycle was parked on the sidewalk leading up to the gymnasium. Did it belong to Miles? Kelly didn't know much about motorcycles; one looked like another to her.

It *could* have been Miles's motorcycle.

She knew of one last door to try and hurried toward the fine arts wing. She found it locked, too.

She turned around and gazed out over the student parking lot next to the fine arts complex. There were more than twenty cars sitting there quietly, waiting for their drivers.

Were there students inside the building this late?

Of course! Kelly remembered there was a production of *The Music Man* in rehearsal. They were obviously practicing late tonight. She could wait for the students to finish and catch the door when they come out.

She positioned herself next to the door, leaning against the brick wall, and waited.

A chilly wind had started to blow. Kelly hunched deeper into her jacket and wrapped her arms around herself for warmth.

The minutes ticked by.

"Come on, guys," Kelly whispered. "Come on out." She hopped up and down for warmth.

Kelly continued to wait.

After more than a half hour, the heavy door was pushed open, and two laughing girls stepped out.

Kelly grabbed the door, and the girls looked at her curiously.

"I forgot my history book," she said, smiling. "Test tomorrow."

The girls laughed and headed down the sidewalk toward the parking lot. Kelly slipped inside.

She knew two entrances to the tunnel: inside the storage room next to the media center and the little door she and Miles had taken the other day.

Kelly was closest to the second door. She hurried, walking purposefully down the hall so as not to draw attention to herself. She didn't want any teachers or custodians who happened to be in the building asking her what she was doing at school so late.

She rounded the corner and started down the short hall where the little door stood at the end.

Six feet away from the door, she stopped in her tracks.

There was a small padlock closed over a new metal hasp.

The custodians must have locked Miles out of the tunnel after they had discovered him and Kelly.

So where *was* Miles? Could he still be down in the tunnel? There were other entrances besides this one. Maybe only this door was locked.

The only other way in that Kelly knew about was the entrance from the storage room next to the media center. Maybe it wasn't locked. She would have to be careful, though. Miles had said that the custodians sometimes have coffee in that room.

Would they be there this late?

Kelly hurried down the long corridor to the other side of the building. She didn't see any students now. They must have all gone home after their rehearsal.

This end of the building was dark. Classroom doors were shut and lights were off. The corridor was quiet and gloomy.

Kelly passed the media center's locked entrance, and she stopped in front of the storage room. She put her ear to the door and listened. Was anyone inside? She couldn't hear anything.

Gingerly, her heart beating hard, she turned the doorknob and opened the door a crack.

Two custodians were shrugging into their coats and heading toward her. Deep in conversation, they didn't notice her.

But they would see her in a moment, unless she could get away quickly and hide. She didn't know whether they were the men who had chased her and Miles through the tunnel or not. If they were, she didn't know whether or not they would recognize her.

She didn't want to wait and find out.

She quickly and quietly closed the door, rushed about ten yards down the hall, and ducked into a recessed classroom doorway. The door was locked, so she plastered herself up against it and froze.

The hallway was dark enough that the custodians

might not notice her when they walked past. At least, she hoped not.

The men apparently hadn't noticed her flight down the hall. They talked in relaxed, conversational tones as they came closer.

Kelly's heart was slamming so hard against her ribs, she was sure they would be able to hear it. She held her position against the door, hardly daring to breathe.

The men got closer and closer, still talking. They were discussing pro football teams, having a friendly argument about whether Chicago or Miami had the better players this year.

Would they see her? If so, would they recognize her and know that she was looking for Miles somewhere in the tunnels? Would they go after him?

Kelly held her breath as they came close.

They passed by, not even seeing her.

She waited until the men had disappeared down the hallway before she dared move. Then she tiptoed out of the doorway and ran back down to the storage room.

She opened the door, stepped inside, and closed the door behind her before she turned on the light switch at her right, flooding the small room with the bright fluorescents overhead.

She spotted the small entrance door to the tunnel on the left side wall. She hurried over to it and tried the small doorknob.

It turned. *It was unlocked!* She opened the door.

Inside, the tunnel was black.

"Miles?" she called softly. "Miles? Are you there? It's me, Kelly."

Miles's face appeared out of the gloom. "Are you alone?"

"Yes."

Miles grinned. "Come on down."

A flashlight popped on in his hand.

Kelly climbed down the stairs and turned to him. Miles's smile disappeared. "What's wrong? You're shaking all over."

"Miles, I have to talk to you."

"What's the matter? What happened?"

"I didn't want to tell you everything until I had proof, but I haven't been able to *get* proof, and tonight somebody tried to kill me."

"Kill you?" His free hand gripped Kelly's arm while he shined the light over her face so he could see her. *"Who? What happened?"*

"First, you have to be calm, Miles, because I need your help."

He nodded. "Okay, tell me what happened."

Kelly told him everything. She told him her suspicions about Jeremy, that *maybe* he was responsible for the robberies, *maybe* the murders. Then she told Miles the rest: her slashed tires, the mysteriously "stuck" freezer door, the threatening note, and finally the horrifying ride home tonight.

"Why didn't you tell me about all of this?" Miles said.

"I didn't know who was doing it for sure. I *still* don't! I think we should go to the police and tell them everything. While they're investigating, I'll avoid Jeremy. Miles, I don't know what else to do. Remember, we aren't *positive* that Jeremy robbed those houses or that he murdered Daryl and Craig."

"There's one way to find out."

"How?"

"Send him a letter."

"A letter?"

"An anonymous letter. It'll say, 'We know about the robberies and murders.' We'll tell him to meet us someplace. If he shows up, we'll know he's scared because he's been found out."

"So what do we do when he shows up? Don't you think he'll come prepared to kill us?"

"We'll be hiding nearby. He'll never see us, but we'll know for sure he's guilty."

"And you promise you'll stay hidden? No trying to get even? No acts of vengeance?"

"I promise. After that, we'll go to the police and then I'll stick close to make sure he doesn't get near you."

"Jeremy will know who the letter's from," Kelly said. "He knows I suspect him of the robberies."

"But the note will say *we* know about him. He'll show up to find out who else, besides you, knows."

Kelly paused. Then she took Miles's hand and squeezed it.

"Okay. I'm scared, Miles, but let's do it."

Chapter 17

"Read it first and make sure it's all right. I'll leave it in Jeremy's car this morning after everybody's gone into the school."

Miles had met Kelly at the Seven-11 about six blocks from Spencer Point High. They wanted to make sure that Jeremy didn't see them together while they planned their meeting with him for tonight.

Standing behind the rack of chips and dip, Miles handed her the folded piece of lined notebook paper. She opened it and read.

We know what you did, Jeremy Watts. We know you're a thief and a murderer. Meet us at the black angel in the graveyard tonight at eleven. If you're not there, we'll go to the police and tell them everything.

"That's good, Miles." She handed the paper back to him. "How are you going to get into Jeremy's car?"

Miles shrugged and looked away. "I'll just—do it."

"You're going to break in, aren't you?"

Miles looked at Kelly. "There's no other way to

get him the note *today,* Kelly. And if we leave it on the windshield, somebody else could pick it up."

"I guess you're right."

"It's not like I'm going to *steal* anything from his car."

Kelly smiled. "You're right. We're *giving* him something."

Miles grinned back. "A note that'll make him swallow his tongue if we're lucky."

Kelly laughed.

"What time do you think we should be at the graveyard?" she asked him.

"At least an hour ahead of time. He might decide to come early, himself."

"I called Ron this morning and told him relatives are visiting and I can't come to work tonight."

"Good."

"I'm missing his special meeting to warn everybody about dangerous pranks at the store. Jeremy'll miss it, too."

"Only if he's guilty."

"I'm getting my new windshield after school, so I can drive tonight. I'll pick you up if you'll give me your address."

"No." His voice was abrupt. "I'll meet you there."

"But I'd be glad to—"

"I'll meet you there."

Why didn't Miles want her to pick him up? Kelly wondered. Was his ego ruffled a little that a girl would pick him up? Was he ashamed he didn't have a car? *Lots* of students didn't have their own cars.

Then she realized what it was. His father. Maybe Miles was worried that his father would be drunk when she arrived.

"Okay," she said. "I'll meet you at ten. Where? At the black angel?"

"No. Meet me at the caretaker's house. We can watch from there."

"Good idea. See you there at ten."

Miles looked at her longingly. "This probably sounds crazy, but I'm looking forward to it."

"I'm scared."

"I know." He grinned. "But I'll get to spend an hour with you before Jeremy shows up."

Kelly smiled back. She stood on her toes and kissed his cheek. "See you later."

Kelly had a hard time sitting still that evening. She had some reading to do for her history class, but she couldn't concentrate on it and gave up after less than ten minutes.

Nana and Grandad were downstairs playing gin rummy, one of their favorite card games. Every once in awhile, she heard one of them shout "Gin!" with a great deal of glee. Kelly smiled to herself. She loved them so much. She was glad they were happy and didn't know where she was going tonight.

She had told them that she had another late-night cram session with Colette tonight. She felt guilty about lying to them again, and she promised herself that after this whole thing with Jeremy was over, she would never tell her grandparents another lie as long as she lived.

Since she was going out to "study" late, she had to stay in her room all evening pretending to work on school assignments. That was okay. She wouldn't have been able to concentrate on gin rummy, anyway, and they would have seen her hands trembling and have known something was wrong.

The clock hands dragged themselves so slowly around the face of Kelly's desk clock, she wondered twice if it had stopped. She called on her phone to get the correct time at 7:06, 7:33, 8:24, and 9:15. The thought of showing up late and Jeremy discovering them made her heart leap into her throat.

Finally, at 9:40, Kelly turned off her desk lamp, stood up, pushed in her chair, and on trembling legs, walked downstairs.

Her grandparents were watching television in the living room. She went to the front closet and pulled out her heavy coat. Even in the caretaker's house, she and Miles would have a chilly wait.

"I'm going to Colette's now, guys," she said, trying to keep her voice steady. She put on her coat.

"Okay," said Grandad without taking his eyes from the screen.

Nana looked up, though, concern written on her gentle face. "Honey, you've been spending an awful lot of late hours studying. I think you're working too hard."

A pang of guilt stabbed at Kelly. "No, not really, Nana. But thanks for thinking about me."

Nana took Kelly's hand. "Do your best in school, honey, but don't neglect your rest. Nothing is more important than your health."

"I know," Kelly said. *Staying alive is an important part of good health,* she thought wryly. "Don't wait up for me."

"I will stay up, unless I just can't keep my eyes open any longer," Nana said with a smile.

"Okay. See you."

Kelly waved good-bye to Nana and Grandad, hoping she'd be home soon after eleven to crawl into her warm, safe bed.

She opened the kitchen door at the back of the house, stepped out onto the porch, and locked the door behind her.

The night was cool and the sweetly smoky scent of burning leaves clung to the air.

This was a night for walking in the park, Kelly thought, not meeting a murderer in the graveyard. She pictured herself strolling hand-in-hand with Miles over leaf-strewn sidewalks. That would have to come later, she realized. After Jeremy had been arrested for robbery and murder. Only then could they relax and live normal lives.

Kelly crossed the backyard to the old barn where her car was parked and pulled open the wide door. Unlike a modern garage, there was no overhead bulb she could switch on. Her station wagon, silent and still, huddled in the barn's black interior.

Kelly never felt very comfortable in the barn at night. She knew there were mice that scurried around inside, and shortly after they'd moved in, they'd seen a bat swooping down from the rafters.

Tonight she was jumpier than ever in the dark. She hurried to her car.

A footstep sounded behind her. She whirled around to see a dark figure step out of the shadows.

"Jeremy!" she gasped.

"Hello, babe," he said. His voice held its usual sneer. "Coming to meet me at the graveyard?"

Chapter 18

Jeremy stood between Kelly and the door, blocking her only way out of the barn. The door was wide, but if she tried to run past him, he could easily take a few steps to either side and grab her.

But even if she *did* get out of the barn past him, where would she run? If she were able to get back to the porch, she'd never get the door unlocked before Jeremy reached her. Besides, she didn't want to endanger her grandparents inside.

These thoughts flitted through her mind in a millisecond, and she realized the only escape was in the car. She stood so close to the driver's door, she could reach out and touch it.

She took a deep breath and grabbed for the car door. She yanked it open, scrambled inside, and locked it just as Jeremy reached the car.

She turned the ignition key, threw the gear into reverse and backed out, the shriek of her tires echoing loudly off the interior walls of the barn.

Outside, she whipped the back end of the car to the side so she could turn around on the gravel drive. In the instant that she was stopped, Jeremy caught up with her, threw himself against the front passenger door, and tried to get inside.

Fortunately for Kelly, it was locked.

Then he grabbed for the back passenger door. It was locked, too.

Kelly threw the car into first gear and stood on the accelerator. The tires spun, spraying gravel, and the car began to move.

The old four-cylinder station wagon didn't have a quick pickup, even with the accelerator pushed to the floor, and it groaned loudly as it heaved itself forward.

"Come on, come on!" Kelly shouted.

In the rearview mirror, Kelly saw a movement at the back of the car. Before she knew what was happening, the rear door to the station wagon was thrown open, and Jeremy leaped inside.

Kelly cried out and the car finally sprang forward. It was much too late, though. Jeremy pulled the rear door closed behind him.

Kelly was now alone in the car with Jeremy. He scrambled to the back seat, banging his knee on something that rang out with a metallic *thunk*.

It was the can of gasoline Kelly'd had sitting in her car since her grandfather had sent her to buy it a week ago. She'd forgotten to take it out of the car.

Jeremy swore loudly and rubbed his knee. Then he vaulted over the backseat and grabbed a handful of her hair with one hand. His other hand came around in front of her.

Snick. She knew what it was before her eyes focused on it. A switchblade. Jeremy held it at her throat.

"Okay, babe, let's go meet your friend."

They had reached the end of her drive at the highway.

"Turn right. We'll meet him—or her—at the graveyard."

"There is no friend," Kelly said. Her throat was dry and constricted. She coughed.

"Yeah sure," Jeremy said sarcastically. "You were going to meet me late at night in the graveyard all alone." He tightened his grasp on her hair. "I said *turn right!*"

Kelly winced with pain, turned the steering wheel, and pulled out onto the highway.

"I was going to watch you from a distance," Kelly said, her breath coming in ragged gasps. "I just wanted to see if you'd come."

"Keep driving and shut up."

Kelly drove toward town, her mind racing. What could she do? How could she warn Miles? Was there any escape?

She thought briefly that she could bash the car into a tree, but that was too dangerous. Besides, if they survived the crash, Jeremy would likely be so angry he'd kill her on the spot.

She kept driving. Maybe she'd think how to escape once they were at the graveyard.

She hoped Miles would be there early. Maybe she could make enough noise as they approached that he would hear them coming and be able to get away for help.

It took twenty minutes to reach the graveyard, and all the while Kelly's heart hammered and her body shook. *This isn't the way it was supposed to happen.*

"Over here," Jeremy ordered. "Park in the lot so we don't attract any patrolling cops."

Kelly obeyed and pulled into the farthest spot in the empty parking area.

"Turn off the motor, but leave the key in the ignition."

Kelly did as she was told. Jeremy got out of the

car first and yanked open the driver's door. He grabbed her coat at the collar and hauled her outside.

"Okay, where were you meeting your friend?"

"I told you, there *isn't* any fr—" Her sentence was broken off when Jeremy hit the side of her head so hard, she spun away, white lights flashing in front of her eyes.

Jeremy whirled her around to face him. He grabbed her coat just under the chin and thrust his face into hers.

"You're *lying!*" His voice was fierce. "You didn't plan this yourself! Now *where* were you going to meet your partner?"

"The black angel," she whispered, her head throbbing with pain. "We were going to meet early, before you got here."

"You'd better be telling me the truth, babe. Get moving."

Jeremy shoved her hard in the direction of the angel statue. She stumbled but managed not to fall down.

The moon, in its last quarter phase, cast only a weak, eerie glow over the graveyard. Faintly visible in the haze surrounding them were the gray tombstones and weather-stripped trees with their wretched, outstretched arms reaching skyward.

Halfway across the graveyard, Jeremy grabbed Kelly and wrapped one arm around her neck.

"We're going to stick together now, nice and close. If you want to stay alive, you'll keep your mouth shut. I don't care if I have to kill you."

As if she needed a reminder, he pressed the sharp blade against the flesh on her neck. A small cry escaped from Kelly before she could stop it, and Jeremy's grip tightened around her shoulder.

"Shut up!" he whispered fiercely in her ear. "Now get moving!"

They walked slowly, veering around tombstones, to the black angel statue.

"Your friend's not here." Jeremy was angry. With his arm still around Kelly's shoulders, the knife at her neck, he shook her hard. "You lied to me, didn't you, babe? Hmmmm? You *lied* to me!"

Kelly cried out and tried to wrestle away from Jeremy, but his grip only tightened, viselike, until she didn't think she could stand any more pain.

"That's enough, Jeremy!" The deep voice boomed out over the graveyard. "Leave her alone."

Miles stepped out of the shadows and into the dim moonlight.

Jeremy's grip on Kelly loosened as he gazed at Kelly's friend.

"Miles Perrin." Jeremy was surprised, but his voice was mocking. "I never would've guessed that you and Goldilocks here would be—what should I say? *Friends?* You don't seem to be her type."

Jeremy obviously knew he had the upper hand, and he was using this opportunity to taunt Miles.

"Father's a drunk, right, Perrin? You live in that old dump at the end of Cod Street."

Even in the dim light, Kelly could see Miles stiffen.

"You're not much better than dear old dad, are you, Perrin?" He jostled Kelly. "What's the matter with you, Goldilocks? You like *trash?*"

Watching Miles's face, Kelly was terrified he would lose his temper and come after Jeremy. Miles was unarmed and would certainly lose in a fight with Jeremy and his switchblade.

But Miles remained cool. "Let Kelly go," he said,

his voice tight but under control. "Let's you and me settle this, Jeremy."

"Oh, but I have both of you right where I want you. Why would I let her go?"

"Well, we found out what we wanted to know, didn't we, Kelly?" Miles said. "Just by showing up, Jeremy, you've admitted to robbery and murder."

"Sure." Jeremy sneered. "I don't mind admitting it. I'm *proud* of it. I've made good money on the stuff I got at those stuck-up women's houses. They think they're so much better than everyone else: patting you on the head like a little dog but never thinking you're any good."

"You killed Daryl, didn't you?" Miles said.

"Yeah, he found out about my operation." He shrugged. "I had to kill him."

"And Craig?"

"Him, too. He was going to tell you everything, wasn't he? It was just a coincidence that I overheard him call you on the office phone. I heard him tell you he knew something about Daryl's hit-and-run. So I knew I had to kill him before he told you about me." He shook Kelly. "But then Goldilocks found out, too."

"You were in the car last night, weren't you?" Miles said. "You tried to kill Kelly by running her out in front of a semi."

"I would've had her, too, if that semi had been going just a little bit faster." Jeremy gazed down at Kelly, who was still held tightly in the crook of his arm. "Oh, well, I'll get the job done tonight."

"You know if you kill Kelly," Miles said, "everyone will know you were the killer."

"How's that?"

"Kelly was mysteriously locked in the freezer at work. Kelly fell down the stairs after the step was cut. If she dies, the cops will be swarming all over the Corner Market."

Jeremy laughed. "You can't pin that stuff on me. In fact, nobody can pin *anything* on me."

Kelly had been listening, waiting for Jeremy to relax a little. She wanted to catch him off guard. When she heard him laugh, she decided it was now or never.

With as much strength as she could muster, she shoved her elbow backward, like a battering ram, into Jeremy's ribs. Even though she was wearing a coat, the force of the blow caught him by surprise. He cried out, momentarily losing his balance, and dropped the knife.

Kelly made a dash away from him and away from Miles. She hoped Jeremy would hesitate, not knowing whether to go after her or Miles. His second of hesitation would give them both a chance to escape.

But Miles wasn't thinking of escape. He rushed toward Jeremy as Kelly stumbled away.

Miles hit Jeremy with his closed fist, and Jeremy staggered backward and fell, his arms outstretched.

"Miles! The knife!" Kelly screamed, for Jeremy's hand had fallen only inches from where the knife lay in the grass. It was so dark, Kelly wouldn't have been able to see it if it hadn't been for the light of the pale quarter moon gleaming dimly off the blade.

Jeremy's hand found the knife and he lunged forward, holding it in front of him.

Both Miles and Jeremy wore dark jackets, and in the blackness of the night, Kelly lost track of which boy was which as they rolled on the ground. Her heart was a cold stone in her throat as she thought of Jeremy's deadly weapon.

Kelly heard a groan and the two stopped moving.

There was a deadly silence. Then one figure stood up over the other and turned to her.

"Now it's just you and me, babe."

Kelly cried out with grief for Miles and terror for herself. She turned and ran as she'd never run before, wildly, in no particular direction.

Get to the car! a voice screamed in her head. *You're going the wrong way!*

She veered off to the right, but realized she would never make it to the car before Jeremy caught up with her.

The caretaker's house was in the distance, and she headed for it.

Yes! she remembered. There were tools inside, hoes and rakes, things that could be used as weapons. She prayed the house would still be unlocked.

She whipped around the side of the house, pushed open the door, scrambled inside, and slammed the door behind her. Groping under the doorknob in the dark, she found a lock and turned it. Hearing the deadbolt slide into place, Kelly collapsed against the door, breathing hard.

She was safe for now. The little house was pretty flimsy, though. It wouldn't take much to get inside if Jeremy really tried.

She took a few fumbling steps until she found a hoe leaning up against the wall. She'd used it to protect herself if she had to.

Remembering the snake the girls had found on their overnight in the graveyard, Kelly decided not to sit on the floor. She remembered the barrel toward the middle of the room and, taking small steps in the dark, moved toward it.

The barrel was still there, and she sat down.

She thought about Jeremy waiting for her in the

barn at home. He must have been there for hours, waiting for her to come out.

She events of the evening rushed through her head, ending with Miles's stabbing.

"Oh, Miles."

Tears filled Kelly's eyes and ran down her face. Miles had been killed trying to protect her. She gave in to the pain welling up in her chest and sobbed.

"Oh, Miles," she whispered. *"I'm so sorry I got you into this. I should have gone to the police."*

Kelly looked around her in the dark. She was relieved but puzzled that Jeremy had not broken a window or kicked in the door to get her.

Where was he?

She got up, clutching the hoe, and peered out the window. The blackness of the night and the film of dirt over the glass prevented her from seeing anything outside.

A faint, familiar odor wafted through the stale air inside the house. Kelly turned toward the smell and drew in a breath.

"Oh, my God."

It was gasoline. Jeremy must have gotten the can from her car.

Wwfff! A large flame leaped up outside the window.

Jeremy had set the house on fire!

Chapter 19

The flames grew higher and hotter and licked at the windows. The small house filled quickly with heavy smoke that stung Kelly's eyes and burned her throat and lungs with every breath.

She wanted desperately to throw open the door and run outside into the cool, fresh air. *But isn't that just what Jeremy wanted her to do?* Wouldn't he be waiting for her just outside, clutching his deadly knife, the knife that was no doubt freshly covered with Miles's blood?

Was it better to die in flames or by the blade? Oh, how she didn't want to choose!

Kelly pulled a tissue out of her pocket and covered her nose and mouth. She coughed violently, and her eyes were stinging and watering so badly she could hardly see.

She remembered reading somewhere that the clearest air in a fire is near the floor, and she dropped to her knees. The smoke was less dense here, but still nearly unbearable.

She crawled to the edge of the room next to the window. Should she break the glass pane? Would she just be providing Jeremy with a way to get in after her? Would he dare come into a burning building?

A tiny puff of cool air brushed her wrist, and scrambling closer, she discovered a small opening in the wall. She pushed her nose to the narrow gap between two of the boards.

This must be how the snakes got inside. The thought flitted through her head and disappeared. She wasn't worried about snakes now. She was worried about staying alive.

It was hard to get enough air through the crack. She moved to one side to reposition herself, and her hand rested on something long and narrow on the floor.

Instinctively, she snatched her hand back as the thought of a dead snake flashed through her consciousness. But then she realized that it was only a short piece of hose.

An idea came to her and she grabbed the hose. It was about two feet long. She squeezed the narrow end through the small opening in the wall, then put her mouth to the other end and gulped in great lungfuls of clean air.

But the air didn't stay clean for long. The wood caught fire under the opening, and as it burned, her hose began to melt and the fresh air became fouled with smoke and burning rubber.

Kelly's lungs felt as if they would explode. There was no possible source of clean air inside the house now.

She realized that now the time had come; she couldn't put it off any longer. She must choose her death: fire or knife?

Kelly's mind grew tired, faint. Her head was pounding. *Maybe it would be easier not to choose, just to give up, go to sleep.*

Something heavy pounded against the door. *Thundered.* The whole house rattled. The noise came a second time, rocking the house on its foundation. Then on the third time, the flimsy door exploded into splinters of wood that flew through the black, churning smoke.

A dark figure towered in the doorway.

It's going to be the blade, Kelly thought vaguely. She didn't care anymore. *Just do it. I'm ready.*

The figure paused for only a moment, then rushed into the house and picked her up off the floor. He carried her out of the thick, heavy blackness and into the clean night air.

Her eyes began to focus.

"Kelly."

She looked up into Miles's face. His face was pinched with pain and worry. He took hold of her hand and she squeezed it. She tried to speak, but her voice wouldn't come.

Instantly, violently, Miles was thrown to one side, and Jeremy was on top of him.

This already happened, Kelly thought. *Jeremy killed him once.* She thought she was hallucinating. Or maybe she was dead, watching her life pass before her eyes, reliving the worst moments just before dying in the fire.

She was aware of the fight going on. She heard the blows, the grunts, and the soft *thuds* as their bodies fell back on the ground. She didn't know how long it went on. She may have passed out for a moment or two.

Her mind began to clear a little as she breathed the fresh air.

She hoped this wasn't an illusion or a death dream. She didn't want to lose Miles twice. Once was more than enough.

Maybe it wasn't a dream. Maybe Miles was still alive. Maybe they had a chance to survive.

146

Miles's face appeared once again.

"Kelly," he said. "I thought you were dead when I found you in the caretaker's house. But you're alive. God, you're *alive.*"

He buried his face in her neck, and weakly, she raised her hand to stroke his head.

"Miles—" Her voice was raspy and hoarse. "What happened to Jeremy?"

"He's unconscious. Come on. I'll carry you to the car."

"Let me try to walk."

Miles helped her to her feet, and leaning heavily against him for support, she took a few tentative steps toward the parking lot. She was dizzy and her head felt as if it were squeezed into a vise, but Miles held onto her tightly.

A movement at their left startled Miles. Kelly felt his whole body jerk as he turned to see what—or who—it was.

"Alice." Miles said her name as she stepped into a soft, silvery pool of moonlight. She held a gun that was leveled straight at them.

"You two don't deserve to live," she said. Her voice was quivering with anger.

"Alice," Kelly said, unable to believe what was happening. "Wh—why are you here?"

Alice took a step closer, aiming at Miles's heart.

"You killed him. You killed Jeremy. He died, and now so will you."

Miles held up his hand. "He isn't dead, Alice, he's unconscious. If you'll let us go get help for him—"

"You're not going anywhere!"

Alice's eyes darted to Kelly.

"You couldn't take your eyes off him, could you?" she said.

"Who?" Kelly's mind was less fuzzy, but Alice wasn't making sense.

"*Jeremy,* who else?" she snapped. "Every time I looked at you, you were watching him."

"I thought you hated Jeremy," Kelly said.

"I *loved* him! And he loved me. At least I thought he did. Then I started to think maybe he was using me to help him with the robberies."

"*You* were involved in the robberies, Alice?" Kelly said.

"We did them together!" Alice said. "I was smaller and could slip in through the basement windows. But then everything changed. Jeremy changed. He started thinking he didn't need me anymore. Oh, he thought he was really hot. He dumped me. Then he started doing the jobs by himself. He knew I wouldn't turn him in because the cops would get me, too."

"Did you help Jeremy kill Daryl?" Miles asked.

"I *planned* that hit-and-run!" Alice said. "But was Jeremy grateful for my saving his hide? Know how he repaid me? He didn't call anymore, he didn't have anything to do with me!"

"What about Craig?" Kelly said. "Did you know he was going to be killed?"

"I thought if I helped Jeremy, he'd see how much I loved him. So I told him Craig had been nosing around, asking everyone questions about the robberies and the hit-and-run. Then he overheard him on the phone with you, Miles."

"So Jeremy killed Craig?"

"I told Jeremy about our graveyard game, but I didn't know he'd come and kill Craig. I was furious when I found out Craig was dead! I *knew* Jeremy had done it. Did he care that *I* was in the graveyard that night? That *I* could be implicated in Craig's death? Of course not! Jeremy's a selfish pig!"

148

"So Jeremy killed Craig after I discovered him playing dead?" Kelly said.

"Yeah, he did it fast and clean, he bragged to me, like that was a big deal. Then he carried away the body before you brought us back to the spot."

"*You* locked me in the freezer, didn't you?" Kelly asked.

"I stuck a chair under the door handle so it wouldn't open."

"Did you cut the stair and send me the note?"

"Yeah, and I cut your tires, too, but I suppose Jeremy took the credit for that," Alice said sarcastically. "He was *nothing* when I met him. I picked him out and built up his self-esteem, protected him—I saw you watch Jeremy take Mrs. Talbot's address and I risked getting caught going through your purse to get that paper—I got myself involved in breaking and entering and *murder* for him, and then he dumped me! I should've killed him myself!"

"If you hate him so much, why are you holding a gun on *us?*" Kelly said.

"I *don't* hate him! I don't want him dead! I'm just so—so *furious* with him. He was so *mean* to me! I wanted to beat him senseless, but I wanted him to love me."

Alice began to sob and the gun in her hands began to tremble.

Kelly vaguely realized she was gripping something in her hand, something that had been with her since she was in the burning house.

The piece of rubber hose. Unconsciously, she'd continued to clutch it as if it were a lifeline, as if it would still provide her with whatever she needed to keep herself alive.

Alice was still crying hard. It was strange, Kelly thought. Alice always seemed so imperious, so strong and able to take care of herself. This was only the second time Kelly had seen a weakness in Alice.

And that's when the idea blossomed in Kelly's mind.

Alice was too far from her for Kelly to rush at her and grab the gun. But the hose . . .

Kelly threw the two-foot hose at Alice's face.

"Snake!" she shrieked. "Look out, Alice, a *snake!*"

Alice, already trembling, screamed and threw her arms up to protect herself from what she thought was a wiggling reptile hurtling through the air at her.

Miles rushed at Alice and grabbed her arms, and Kelly took the gun from her hand.

Alice slumped over, defeated. Even the anger seemed to have left her. She looked small and withered, like a balloon that had lost most of its air.

"It's over," Kelly said to her. Alice didn't look up or respond.

Kelly gazed up at Miles, took a big breath and let it go. "It's really *over.*"

Chapter 20

"What a beautiful Saturday!" Kelly said, kicking through a drift of leaves in the city park.

The chilly autumn air was whispering of the coming winter, but the sky was a warm, sunny blue. Kelly and Miles, dressed in jeans and heavy jackets, walked hand-in-hand under the tall oaks, crunching leaves and acorns under their feet.

"Your grandparents aren't going to like me, you know," Miles said, gazing at two children playing on the swings.

"Of course they'll like you!" Kelly grinned. "You saved my life, Miles. They can't wait to thank you. You're a hero!"

"No, but after they meet me—"

"Then they'll *really* like you."

"We come from different worlds, Kelly."

"So? My grandparents will only care that you're a nice person. You wait and see."

"I hope you're right."

"I'm just so glad you weren't badly hurt," Kelly said. "What did the doctor say about your stab wound? Didn't you have an appointment with him yesterday afternoon?"

"Yeah. He said the emergency room doc did a

good job of stitching me up and said I was real lucky that the knife didn't hit any important organs."

"We were both lucky. If you hadn't come to get me in the caretaker's house when you did, I wouldn't be here."

Miles slipped his arm around her. "I don't even want to think about that."

They walked to a green park bench at the edge of the playground and sat down.

"I wonder how Jeremy's doing?" Kelly said.

"I don't care how Jeremy's doing. I hope he gets what's coming to him."

"The detective I talked to said he'll be charged with arson, kidnapping, and two counts of attempted murder. There may be more charges later, after their investigation is complete."

Miles nodded. "That ought to put him away for a while. What about Alice?"

"She's being held, too. I think she's going to be sent to a psychiatrist before anything's decided about her." She squeezed Miles's hand. "You were right about Alice, you know."

"Yeah. I couldn't figure out why you wanted to hang around with her and her friends."

"She seemed awfully sour and I didn't like her very much, but I sure didn't think she was capable of murder."

"People can surprise you."

"Miles, Colette really *is* nice. I want you to get to know her."

"No thanks. I'm sure she's already made up her mind about me."

"I talked to her yesterday, and she wants us to double with her and a date sometime. She says she was dumb to prejudge you without ever getting to know you."

Miles nodded but didn't say anything.

"You might want to get to know her, too, before you decide whether you like her or not," Kelly said softly.

Miles suddenly grinned and shook his head. "Yeah, okay, I guess I'm guilty of the same thing."

"Well, so was I! I thought you'd stolen that helmet without even considering that you might have gotten it some honest way."

"Yeah, that reminds me—"

"What?"

"You still have that helmet?"

"Yes."

"You going to ride with me on my bike?"

Kelly grinned. "Sure. But no wheelies, okay?"

Miles grinned back. "Okay. But you've got to take risks sometimes."

"Are you *kidding?* I've taken enough risks in the past ten days to last me for the rest of my life!"

Miles pulled her close. "You're right about that, Kelly. You're sure right about that."

He kissed her gently.

A leaf fluttered through the air and landed on Miles's shoulder. Kelly picked it up and gave it back to the breeze.

She sighed contentedly and snuggled into Miles's warm jacket. Maybe Spencer Point wasn't going to be so bad after all.